I0615644

EVERY WOUND IN THE WORLD

100 stories of exactly 500 words each

By Jim Marcus

. . . .

PULSEBLACK

Every Wound in the World
100 stories of exactly 500 words each
by Jim Marcus

September, 2024

This book is set in Lato Regular 9/13
Titles in Lato Heavy 16/20

Cover:
The Wound Man
by Jim Marcus 2023

Foreward by Donna Lynch
Edited by Janet Valle

ISBN 979-8-9917282-2-5

This is dedicated to all the children in my life
that have made it worth living

Index

Forward

....

For Every Wound, a Voice
By Donna Lynch

I wrote to Jim as I was reading these stories and asked if he found it bothersome or unhelpful when people note comparisons to other artists' work. He said he didn't, which was good, because I—even as a writer—didn't know if I could convey the range of emotions I felt while reading this collection without drawing parallels to how I felt about Ray Bradbury's The Illustrated Man, and a few times, Clive Barker's Books of Blood. I also remember similar sensations coming over me during various episodes of Black Mirror.

There's always a risk when you do this.

If Jim disliked any of the above, if the reader disliked them, then I may have hurt more than I helped (though I have some thoughts about anyone who'd talk shit about Ray Bradbury).

But for anyone who may have formed an opinion based on my comparisons—know that these stories are not copies of, nor do they even feel like they are consistently paying homage to, any of the aforementioned collections.

They just hit me in the same internal space.

Much like those modern classic works, these 500-word pieces make me feel afraid of the unknown and of the potential of a tenuous tomorrow, and at the same time, hopeful and less alone in the universe.
We are presented with stories of the tech we know is coming, as well as the tech we can only imagine.

We are shown the world we may be looking at in both the near and the far future.

But in all of this, be it progress or regression, our humanity remains the same at its core. We are fragile and strong, selfish and compassionate, self-aware and delusional, profound and shallow, and all the other paradoxical elements that comprise us.

These are brisk yet impactful stories of love, survival, horror, and acceptance; dreaming from other dimensions; unconscious heavens, personal hells, deities, aliens, and places unstuck in time; stories from the cities, from the future, from the earth, and from the sea, all so impressive by the very nature of their plots, but even more remarkable in their diversity.

And as I read—noting that diversity—I was struck by something unexpected: Often in art, when you know the creator, you can hear their voice, or see them in the creation.

But I don't hear Jim in this collection.

I hear the voices of the characters, the unseen narrators from the multitudes of cities and various realms.

Knowing the author, I shouldn't have been surprised.

We once acknowledged the dual nature of ourselves and our beliefs, but we know now that nearly everything exists on a spectrum, broad and wonderfully non-binary.

Such is the nature of his stories. They have their own identities, and their own unique place on that spectrum.

And in hindsight, I've come to realize that it wasn't that I didn't hear his voice among the pages.

I was just hearing some of his other voices for the very first time.

Introduction

· ·

Refracting Reality

By Jim Marcus

I grew up reading comic books. No doubt most people who have written three books of short stories in a row likely did.

In comics, continuity is a unique modulator. It can be used, abused, twisted, deformed, reset, and managed in so many ways that it would drive Voltaire crazy.

At the same time, my Mother was watching soap operas. Many soap operas. It had become clear that I wasn't going to be able to talk to her about much if I didn't have the basic vocabulary, so I watched All My Children, General Hospital, etc. I noticed that the two mediums had some interesting methods in common.

There was a technique that my friends, also rabid comic fans, and I had noticed about comics. A new kind of narrative structure. We called it "refracting." It's something that happens when the same event is described from different perspectives and it is fundamentally changed. The hero in one retelling may not be so heroic in another. The bad guy may gain some story-driven sympathies when we see their motive, their reason. Both soap operas and comics also had a wildly engaged and energetic fan base, one that dipped into fanfiction when they felt passionate.

It became clear that there were three different parts that made up the "Real world" I might see or read. Firstly, there was what was in the text of that story, verbatim. Secondly, there were the implications of that text, in comparison to other stories in that same universe, contextualized by what we knew about the characters and situations elsewhere.

Thirdly, there was the deep pool of growing "fan fiction" in the mind of the reader, generated by passion and commitment to continuity and logic.

In both comics and soap operas, fans were co-creators.

In college, I wrote a dissertation on Shakespeare's "Romeo and Juliet" that posited that the two lovers were actually brother and sister, predicated on an infidelity in the past that had left the Montagues and Capulets at odds forever after. As a member of the clergy, the only one who didn't know was, of course, the Friar. Suggestions from the text, implications from other writings, coupled with my own "Fan Fiction," gave this theory a sort of life of its own. To me, suddenly the text made much more sense.

I'm not Shakespeare, so please, lower your expectations accordingly, but, at the same time, see if it is possible to read the three hundred entries in the first three books of stories with that idea in mind. There are a-ha moments for you to discover, if you are willing to read closely. There are gray spaces for you to fill in if you engage and try to use your own imagination. And there are worlds connected by natural laws, people, places, and events.

Like a time-traveling subtractionist, you may have to read the reality around you a bit and determine where you belong in it...

And decide where your own ideas fit in.

1 - Each Night When the Baby Hums

Cynthia was almost six months old but it seemed like she had already learned how to put her father right to sleep. David couldn't help it. When the baby hummed all day and then sort of purred at night, it was a unique auditory experience.

It was almost like she was vibrating. She was a happy girl. Which made David and his wife, Mona, especially happy because of where this journey had begun.

Cynthia was supposed to have died in the womb. Mona was crushed, despondent, when she couldn't feel the baby kicking anymore at thirty two weeks. David wasn't a religious man, but he knew Mona needed to not feel alone. He encouraged her to pray, to wish, and hope. And sure enough, a week later, she felt the baby kick again.

The doctors didn't know what had happened. But they encouraged the young couple to keep positive and to keep planning. And, sure enough, on the exact day she was expected, Cynthia was born, a quick labor and a beautiful baby girl.

Right from the start she seemed like an old spirit. She was content to just hum all day long- these half songs that she couldn't have possibly heard. When he pushed her in the stroller David could feel the vibrations of her gentle humming. And then, he couldn't even count the number of times that her soft vibrating purr had put him to sleep lying next to her at night, Mona right behind them.

David loved spending time with his daughter, but it did seem like, over the last few months, Mona had gotten more and more distant. He tried to include her when he and the baby played, but she seemed preoccupied.

Like tonight, in the bathroom, spending so much time just staring into the mirror while David and Cynthia prepared for bed. David called out to her as he realized that today was the 22nd - Cynthia's exact six month birthday. Mona seemed distraught and he tried to spread his own bright mood in her direction to put her at ease. He told Mona how happy he was for his baby.

Then, David saw a look in her eyes he had never seen before. Was she sick? He put his hand on her stomach and that familiar hum seemed to have gotten louder. He felt a flutter under his fingers. He pressed down slowly and the skin on Cynthia's belly gave way, almost pulling his hand into the hole it had left in her stomach, filled with thousands of tiny buzzing insects, each one more alien looking than the last.

David screamed and pulled back, the insects swarming him as her eyes shone red behind the swarm.

David flailed while the insects ate away at his face. He called out to Mona, 'I thought you said you prayed to Jesus..."

Mona huddled in the corner, waiting for her baby to finish eating. "I did, David, at first. But Jesus was the one who didn't listen."

2 - Garaki's Genie

....

Everyone should know their limitations and their purpose.

This is the unlikable phrase Daniel Garaki lived by. He grew up poor but he wouldn't stay that way. It seemed like everything he really wanted, he was able to make happen.

In the third grade he had met the girl of his dreams, Hannah. And in her whole life she had never loved anyone but him. Daniel used to love telling people she was a virgin, untouched except by him.

The right job, the right home. The right friends.

It wasn't hard for Daniel to have whatever he wanted.

Unfortunately, Daniel didn't care about being loved by people. So he wasn't. His employees disliked him. His family thought he was pompous and overreaching, banal and cruel. Even his beautiful virgin wife, Hannah preferred the company of baristas and nail salon employees over him.

One day, and I say it like this because this is a bit of a fairy tale, she met Lowell, the Barista that would change her life.

Sort of.

In reality, fucking Lowell only really served to bring her out of her self-imposed fog. But it was fun. And she really did need to wake up.

One Saturday she brought Lowel down to the basement to avoid prying eyes as she explored some two decades of relevant fetishes she had missed out on, and saw a tiny door leading to a crawl space. She detached from Lowell and the two of them went spelunking, only to find a miniature man shriveled and dead on the floor. On the wall next to him the man had scrawled his story as he laid there, bleeding out.

As a child Daniel had found the Genie and ensured, through a series of wishes, that everything he touched would go his way. He made sure that he would regenerate, that he lived long enough to enjoy it all. And then he murdered that little genie.

So Hannah and Lowell made their own decisions. Which began with suffocating Daniel uncomfortably to death in his sleep.

And that is where Daniel, or at least parts of Daniel, discovered their limitations...

And their purpose.

Skin accounts for about fifteen percent of your body weight. The average adult has approximately twenty-one square feet of skin, which weighs nine pounds. But since part of his enchantment was that Daniel always healed, his brain dead body had a near endless amount of skin, Skin that had been enchanted to give him anything he touched, anything he wanted.

Hannah realized that she could stretch that skin over wooden frames and make canvases to paint on. She would dry them and color them black so no one would know. But they wouldn't be normal paintings.

She visualized that genie, dismembered for his power in Daniel's crawlspace. She imagined the genie enjoying the irony of all of this. She wished that he was still here. He might enjoy the opening of her new project, Garaki's Art Supply Store.

Where dreams come true.

3 - Thirty

....

"Just back off for a minute, sir," The police officer said, while blocking Jackson in a corner.

"Look, we don't have much time. I'll show you, upstairs then you can just take me in if you want."

The officer looked at the older couple who were shaking their heads, "Absolutely not. That's our bedroom."

Jackson tried to make a break for it when the second cop tackled him. He leaned in and tried to calm the younger long-haired Jackson down."Look, man, let's take a deep breath..."

The couple interjected, "can you get him out of here?"

The first officer asked, "He said he used to live here, so he doesn't anymore?"

Jackson was itching to explain, "No, my mom and I used to rent the upstairs here. The back room was my room. Just go up there and look out the window." Jackson was panicked and the officers wanted to know why.

Ray, the older man, pulled his wife Sandra closer. "We just want to enjoy our last few years. This can't happen, officers, you understand that. We only let him in in the first place because he used to be a nice young boy."

And as that young boy, Jackson used to stare out that back window every day. Until he noticed something impossible.

It seemed like the world you could see from the back window was about thirty hours ahead of the world you saw through the front. It was impossible to ignore. If it had been a day, twenty-four hours, or two days, forty-eight, he might not have noticed. But the window consistently showed a world thirty hours in the future.

And when it showed Scotty Micek sneaking around the back way to come beat him up after school, he pushed against it and broke it. That was the only time that a prophecy made by the window hadn't come true.

"We have to break the window."

"This is insane," Sandra rolled her eyes.

"In 30 hours, it shows it. It's all black. Everything is gone"

"Are you buying this?" Ray smiled at them.

Jackson's shoulders sank and there was a tear in his eye. "Please. I beg you. Break the window. Or just go up and see it. See what I saw, when I snuck up there. That's all I'm asking you."

The first officer turned to face the couple. "What are we going to see if we look out that back window?"

Ray turned in one quick motion, severing the throats of both the officers with his tongue, snaking out 6 feet in front of him. As they dropped to the floor, Sandra crawled to them and wordlessly licked at the blood, her own tongue long and sinewy.

Ray moved close enough to smell his breath. It smelled like turpentine as his eyelids fluttered left to right, exposing insectoid eyes

Jackson heard the old man's feral hissing as his throat ripped open pouring blood out onto the ground, and then everything just went black.

4 - The Angel of Santa Veranza

Mauricio found the angel in his pool on the night of the seventeenth of August, laying face down in the water, presumably drowned. He fished him out and dragged his seemingly lifeless body into the painting studio he had made for his wife in the garage.

He was remarkably light.

Mauricio and Helena stared at him on the paint splattered tarp and tried to figure out if they believed in angels. It had been a strange couple of years and, honestly, no one was as credulous as they might have been in 2030...

Before the world just went to shit.

Helena had made the case that if he was, indeed, some kind of angel that he would likely still be alive. Surely a few feet of old pool water couldn't kill one of god's minions? That was a good argument on this side, for lack of belief

On the other hand, she said, he fucking looked like an angel.

Mauricio found on that hand an appealing argument. The angel was light, presumably with hollow bones, over seven feet tall, thin and stretched out, like a pappardelle noodle on a roller, and just as white.

Suddenly Mauricio began to miss good Italian food.

The angel started to stir and Helena decided that it should eat as she ran off to make a grilled cheese sandwich and some of those airfryer potato things they actually ate with every meal now.

Mauricio secretly wished they had figured out how to make ketchup as he tried to help the angel up.

Now, you can believe this story or not. But it was a credible one to Mauricio. The Angel told him he had been thrown out of heaven for choosing to defy god. That part of the story certainly sounded familiar. But the reason why was alarming.

For very long-lived intelligences, there are long periods of times where they sort of "switch jobs". And after 4 billion years of being good, God just decided...

Well, to be the other thing.

Mauricio considered all this while the angel bit into the sandwich delivered by his wife. The timeline matched this hell on earth.

The angel began to buckle in pain. His eyes darted to Mauricio as he silently pleaded but there was nothing he could do. A stream of light shot from the crack that opened down his body, from the start of his temple to his feet, dissecting him into, seemingly, two perfectly symmetrical halves while he slunk to the floor.

Helena looked at Mauricio who had begun to retch in horror. She resisted the urge to help him up as she stepped over the now rotting angel. She had always been a woman of faith but watching the blessed water infused into that grilled cheese sandwich destroy the fallen angel made her more confident than ever that she could snap her husband's neck as God had told her to in the kitchen not five minutes before.

She smiled and prayed a little bit.

5 - The Strike of the Lamplighters

....

"As I start this, I hope you will all bear with me a little. It's a roundabout, but the car eventually makes it into the garage."

The crowd of press members mumbled for a minute then died now as they all prepared themselves for Nora's special brand of nonsense. Salme shook his head at Levi. There was no way they would make their 6pm deadline for the last online posting. He desperately wished the small dark woman behind the podium would just hurry this shit up.

Thank you.

She continued.

"Many of you have dogs. And you are busy busy people. So you rely on a dog walker. You probably don't think about it much. You don't have to. But what if the Dogwalkers disappeared tomorrow?"

Salme raised his hand. The woman looked palpably annoyed. "Yes?"

"Salme Ryan, The Post online. I'm afraid a lot of us are lost. Can you explain what a…" as he looked down at his notes and turned a page, " … lamplighter is, please?"

The woman's name was Nora Flench. We should probably remember that for later. Nora Flench. She answered, slightly annoyed, "I was going to… ok, your colleagues from the National Enquirer know all about this, but it may not be common knowledge elsewhere. A lamplighter is a person who is, in all other ways a normal human. But it's their job to help people… well…fall in love."

The short round of laughter that erupted fundamentally changed the entire tone of the room. It was clear that this was now one of THOSE kinds of press events. Levi clicked his recorder off.

After that, many of their colleagues stood up and asked smallish questions. How many lamplighters were there? How did you get to be one? And the big question, I guess.

"So why are you going on strike?"

Nora took a deep breath, " Not only are we unrecognized, YOU, the people out there, make it harder every day to do our job. You think you can meet someone to love on a program on your phone? Or some speed dating event? Or the produce section of the supermarket?"

Nora got angrier as she recounted the difficulty in her craft, ending with the proposition that lamplighters would be taking a step back until they were recognized for their value to society.
Salme laughed it off and waited for the circus sideshow to end. He tried to imagine how he might write this up.
As the room started to clear and Salme had made his way toward the North Exit, he realized something. The burning passion he had felt his whole life for journalism, the written word, the news, it wasn't there anymore. He really had no interest in getting back to the office. He looked at Levi, who seemed to be having an epiphany of his own. Levi paused.

"Hey, man. You want to just get a couple beers next door?"

Salme thought for a minute.

He couldn't think of any reason why not.

6 - Settle Down

....

When you finally understand something, you write about it.

You try to explain it. You tell other people, because that's what we do. We are a social species after all.

And when we learn something that changes everything we know and think and feel, that is a good thing, right?

My name is Tau Liveri which means, in the language of my people, "the range- the area." It speaks to openness and travel and liberation. It's a beautiful name, really,

And it's deeply ironic right now.

You see, I was born to travel.

Even more than most of my race, a people that were designed, by nature, to be the most efficient travelers in the universe.

I not only have the organs in my body, in places humans do not, that process energy in ineffable ways, allowing me to close my eyes and visualize a place, or time, I'd like to be, anywhere in the universe...

...And then be there.

But I also have the will to push that as far as I can. To visit places far outside the range of what is possible for my people.,

And not only do I have these instincts, ones that are nascent in many species, to teleport, to remove myself when danger strikes, I also have other tools provided by my genetics to stave off harm, plus my own substantial training.

My people, in times of distress, begin to change, to morph their appearance, to look like the dominant species where we are. It helps us blend in and escape danger. As well, we can see in space and time specific distances, while we learned to build machines that can see even farther. As I say, the most efficient travelers in the universe, and I, probably one of the most efficient of all of them,

So why, I wondered, over and over again while younger, do my people hide so much? Why do we keep to ourselves? Why do we huddle in our own galaxy as though timid and reclusive? I suppose if you were reading very thoroughly, it's already become clear to you, although it took me a while.

I am often dense, I suppose.

I appeared here on Earth around this time last year. I looked very different. Human eyes work differently than ours, human hands, human mouths. I appeared in the middle of a war, in a way, a massacre, the foot soldiers of some alien race beating down the humans in the street. My outward appearance began to reflect these aliens right away, my body recognizing them as the new dominant species.

But then something unexpected happened. The humans won. Overnight their victory was so decisive that these aliens ran scared as fast as their warp ships could take them. Over the course of the next few days, I lay in bed as my physiology radically attempted to compensate.

I became more human. And the longer I was here, even more. The organs I used for travel disappeared...

7- The Ambassador

....

"The Ambassador has arrived, sir"

Vladek sighed and tried to look presidential. All he managed was to look annoyed. He waved, "Let him in." He tried to remember to pronounce the man's name - Ntshamiseko Udu. What the fuck was wrong with these idiots from these shithole countries that they couldn't just name their kids normal things?

The blind Ambassador stepped into the Oval office, dressed in a black suit with a colorful African sash draped over one shoulder. He reached to shake the president's clammy hand.

At six foot three, the Ambassador towered over most men. For all his inadequacies, however, Vladek was quite a tall man. For once, he looked straight across the room into another man's eyes. Ntshamiseko's eyes were white and unseeing.

"What can I do you for," Vladek opened. Maybe this would be quick.

Ntshamiseko sat, indicating that it would likely not be quick. He steepled his fingers and began.

"Do you know who I am?"

Vladek had been given some intel. In some of the countries of Africa, this man was considered some kind of hero. He was called Vululami, another annoying fucking name no one could remember. Vladek puffed up his chest a bit. "Yes, I have intelligence all over the world. Let's say not too much escapes me."

The ambassador reached out with his abilities and tried to really see this man. This president was cruel, shallow, cold, a racist bully who pushed people around just to see them jump. He was forceful and brutal to women, facile and falsely charming to important men, and oblivious to children and those who couldn't help him. And his policies reflected all that. His cruelty, his ignorance, his lack of common decency.

Ntshamiseko told him all that.

Vladek fumed. "Well, hey, In that case, Mr. Hero, why don't you get the fuck out of my office."

The hero of the people known as Vululami continued, "I tried to see what kind of man you were and what could be done about you. But my abillties work better like this. And I see you better. I will leave." He reached out and grasped the President's hand again. Vladek took it wanly.

"My people can walk you out, asshole." with his other hand, Vladek reached out to press the buzzer to one side right on his desk. He never reached it.

A magnetic pulse originated in the Ambassador's palm, traveling up Vladek's arm to his brain. It gathered like a storm cloud around the walnut sized tumor in the President's frontal lobe. Both men felt a slight shock as the pulse eradicated the tumor by ripping apart the iron in the blood that fed it, purging Vladek's brain.

The President sat down.

As the Ambassador left, President Vladek rose again, pulling open the blinds on the window.

He had no idea why it had been kept so dark in here. The sun streamed in and he considered what a beautiful day it was going to be.

For everyone.

8 - Perala the Mermaid

Once upon a time, in the wild ocean near the Azores lived a mermaid by the name of Perala.

She had strong gills, tiny fins along her hips and a magnificent tail whose scales would reflect the colors around them, chameleon-like, taking on the greens, blues, and even violets of the surrounding water.

She swam with her sisters in untamed ocean currents and laughed along with them. Besides her home, her people, and play, there was nothing she thought twice about.

Until the ship came.

The Euridice was a trading ship, populated by young men wanting to kickstart their fortunes and get a head-start on building toward a life of leisure. It carried expensive spices to and from the islands and every man aboard was obsessed with their mission.

Except Adão, often seen leaning over the edge of the ship, pining for his life back home, bemoaning how his father had attached him to this crew, to find his wealth, against his will.

Perala realized she loved Adão the second she saw him, focused more on the lapping waves than his own work. She smiled and waved.

And he waved back.

For weeks, you could find them both at the docks, every day, talking, laughing, staring into each other's eyes. And then it was time for Adão's ship to move on.

He knew he would be back in a month, but after that, it would be hard to return. The two wept as they tried to figure out what to do, how to be together. And as his ship slowly pulled away, Perala knew what she had to do.

She swam to the bottom of the Atlantic, not far from the islands, near Lisbon, where great temples to the gods were stretched out for miles undersea in any direction. She knew the one she wanted. Without hesitation, she swam lithely into the beautiful temple made to Alitha, the goddess of love. She prostrated herself in front of her holy space and begged Alitha to do whatever she could to let her be with Adão for good.

She went into detail about their love, told her all about him. But she knew she could never live like this in Adão's world. She begged the goddess to make her a human woman to be with the man she loved.

And that's when Alitha appeared. She put her arms around Perala gently and held her close. She kissed her forehead and spoke softly in her ear as she explained that she could not do what the young mermaid wanted. For as the goddess of love, she knew that true love lets you love yourself, too, for who you really were.

And Perala was perfect the way she was.

The young mermaid cried often as he watched Adão over the years, marry, and raise beautiful children,

And hundreds of years later, she saw his beautiful descendants, successful, happy.

And one day, she returned to the temple to thank Alitha for her own happy ending.

9 - The Life and Times of Demondog

What a lot of the media gets wrong about Demondog is that he's really just a dog.

He's not a de-evolved human super or a demon. He's just a very very large, feral, powerful, vicious, super strong dog who can fly and shoot lasers from his eyes.

Simple.

He was bred and raised by supervillains, and he helped them to terrorize Victory city until the handsome hero known as Prototype stopped him.

So now he sat, fuming, angry, in chains in the sub basement of the Victory city super prison known as the Boot.

Which is German for "boat."

I don't know, I have no idea why they named it the Boot. I'm sure it wasn't that. I just remember that movie.

The guard looked confused, "Aren't you Prototype?"

Anthony Pressman smiled and shook his hand. "Yes, I am. Nice to meet you?"

"Did you just call yourself 'Handsome'?" asked the guard with a wink.

"Tell me I'm not." Anthony slapped the guard on the back like an old friend.

"Well, you have all the paperwork. He's yours. But why does a superhero want a super villain dog?" the guard asked, putting on the titanium laced gloves he wore when he went anywhere near the cages. He loved his hands.

Anthony moved into the cell and gently pet the animal. Demondog flew into a rage, ripping and clawing at him. He tried to eat his head and tear his body in pieces with his terrifyingly big claw-tipped paws.

Luckily, since birth, the hero known as Prototype had been invulnerable to all forms of harm. Just as it had been when he helped capture him, there was nothing that Demondog could do to hurt him.

Anthony Pressman held the dog closely as he flew over the city to the outskirts hundreds of miles away. He didn't let go when they landed on the sprawling farm that his family now owned, complete with a reinforced barn and two hundred acres of wide open space.

Anthony could see the tiny burn marks around the dog's neck where some insanely powerful device had been used to torture him. He could feel the lash marks and scars on his back, under his fur. And every day, he stayed with him, working, training, showing him love.

Eventually Demondog responded very well to "DD." The people they saved together seemed to find that name more approachable. DD was comfortable with the matching bandana Anthony had bought, in the same crimson and gold as his Prototype costume.

Nearly eighteen months after he had picked him up from the Boot, Anthony tossed a piece of steak as far into the air as he could. DD licked his lips and looked at him for a second then leapt upward.

Anthony considered building a home for dogs that no one else could help, run by his invulnerable self - dogs that had been weaponized, brutalized, hurt until they just wanted to hurt others.

Because there's no such thing as a bad dog.

10 - The Sound of Mummy's Voice

....

Dr. Jennifer Ngaro had worked very hard to get her team to just call her "Jen" for the last ten months. If she had to record her findings, she would note, for the record, that it hadn't worked.

"Dr, Ngaro, the dilator is connected."

"It's J - nevermind. Thank you, Francis."

The Ironic thing was that Frances Cooper, the young girl deferring to her so hard, was the real genius behind this project. Jen had been an Egyptologist now for over thirty years, but she was afraid that her days of new discovery were over. It seemed like every secret ancient Egypt had it had given up years ago, to the thousands of her colleagues who persevered and struggled every day to learn.

And Dr. Ngaro's discipline was even more narrow. She was fascinated by how the ancient pharaohs led, how they generated the incredible loyalty they did.

Why people killed and died for them,.

Frances was much younger. And her specialities were all over the place. From AI to 3D printing, she had proven invaluable to the expedition.

And this device was her baby.

The Dilator was their own fabricated version of the voice of the Pharoah they were here to study, Djoser, the son of King Khasekhemwy and Queen Nimaathap, and the successor to Nebka. His step pyramid was the oldest giant monument built in the area.

And they knew virtually nothing about him.

Frances had helped to use AI to recreate everything that WAS known about him, along with everything they discovered along the way, supplemented by guesses from the computer based on the region. That was genius. They were building his personality.

But even more genius was the Dilator itself. It was a 3D printed version of his voicebox and larynx, meant to help simulate the exact sounds made by his mummified throat, when he was alive. This is the closest they would ever get to hearing Djoser's own words in his own voice. And it had never been done before.

Freances finished the calibrations. "We're ready to go, Dr."

Jen turned to her with affection, "You know we're actually partners now. In all this. I could never have done this without you. Both of our names are going to be together in the history books. Maybe just 'Jen' is okay"

Frances smiled. She adored Dr. Ngaro and was deeply grateful for everything she learned. She switched the machine on.

The computer's face lit up as the voice echoed throughout the complex, driven through the dilator. There was something familiar about it that Jen just couldn't identify, but, as well, something alien, something behind the voice.

"Hello, Dr. Ngaro. It's very nice to meet you…"

Jen's eyes glazed over and she grew silent as she heard the thing behind the voice. Like a whisper. A secret. It said, "open"

She listened captivated as every single door in every room of the building and across the outlying town hummed and swung open.

And then it said something else.

11 - 22 Days

....

I'm sorry. Are you using that?

No, the pen. I don't... The pen on the desk doesn't work

It's all the little yellow post it notes. You know? You have to initial all of them and then sign.

Yeah, this is... I guess this is what giving up looks like. You're going through a divorce? That really sucks, man, I'm sorry.

Oh, mine? Why is it so small? Well I guess I'm going through a divorce, too. Except, my wife was, how do you say it? Fictional.

Yes, like a cartoon character. Exactly like that.

Well, I remember walking with her, holding hands, something I don't usually like very much. And she was talking, kind of babbling, actually, and I loved it.

We'd been together for about 14 days. It was just two weeks since I slammed into her right at the door of the restaurant.

And. We walked by this Key shop, you know? And the sign on the front, it said, I swear to god, "Keys made- they work" And she starts going on about what a great piece of advertising that was. Like, this is the bar, right? The only thing a key really needs to do is to open a goddamn door. What a miracle of modern advertising this was. And I laughed. And then it sort of came out. After I laughed. She looks at me and she whispers, "I love you." And this was 14 days.

22 days altogether. Married? Married for 5 days.

On the 15th day we go to the Sybaris, you know the place? It's like some ridiculous lovers' hotel. But it was amazing. We talked all night. We agreed. When does that happen, right?

Day 16 we curl up all day and we read to each other. Because it's raining like fuck all. You know, the rain? Trapped in the house. Reading Tolkein back and forth and doing the voices, you have to do the voices. The accents. All of it.

And the next day we get up like we're hypnotized, and we go to city hall and we just do it. And the next 5 days are just…. I just felt like a person,. Like a living thing. Like I belong and so does she. And it's weird. My fingers were tingling. I felt healthy. That's stupid, I know.

Me and Nicole.

Except there was no Nicole. Nicole Jennings, married name, who gives a shit, because there is no one by that name. She's a cartoon. She's Wile E. Coyote. And I answered the police, every question, Every Goddamn question. This form says they get to read all this. In humiliating detail.

And you know what's so crazy? The bank account she cleaned out? 4,712 dollars. I would have given it to her. The TV? Like 400. I would have sold it for her. All of it. The math. I'm not rich. I'm not anything.

For another 22 days? All of it. All of it.

Here's your pen.

12 - The Song of Remembrance

Ayliha's grandmother had died of Alzheimer's not long before she had the idea. She started on a project to find a tone, a sound, that would help prime the brain to remember, to maintain the precious data it had captured.

It would be a tool to help stave off Dementia.

We forget the role that hearing loss has on dementia. Hearing loss, even a small amount, can lead to isolation. Even to situations where the person just feels like it's too exhausting to constantly try to hear and understand. So they pull away. They become quiet.

Then, they disassociate. They become an alien observer in their own life, in their own world. And from there it's just a step or two into dementia.

Ayliha knew this all too well. But why sound?

Ayliha needed something not too invasive. Something non surgical. Hopefully even something non medical. Something that was easy for the millions of families dealing with this issue. And sound was her thing. She grew up in a musical household. Between her mother's frequent Operatic performances at the Lyric Opera and her father's garage band engagements at the bar around the corner, she felt like she was always sitting there for one or another of her family performing.

And she admitted that putting out her own singles under her band name was extremely satisfying.

She knew music and sound.

And what it could do.

She imagined a wave, cycling through the frequencies of human beta waves. It would resonate along with the waves, much like how a tuning fork resonates along with objects vibrating at the same frequency. And when the wave faded, the memory would be amplified stronger, more powerful.

That is what she hoped would happen.

And so she built her machine. The first version was elaborate and made from metal tines that operated as tuning forks. And when she turned it on, she could feel the tone as it resonated against the edges of her memory. But it wasn't strong enough.

She had the idea, eventually, to build an app. It would transmit the sound in a way that wasn't reliant on materials. It would perpetuate the sound longer, louder, in ways that, if it worked, would do the trick.

The sound would attach itself to memory.

Ayliha finished the last few lines of the app and compiled it. She connected it, via bluetooth, to the small orange JBL speaker in front of her and hit "go".

The pilot carrier wave rang through the entire house. It was soothing, calming, even. And it captured Ayliha's imagination as it lulled her to rest. It was a beautiful, almost perfect sound.

She felt refreshed. She felt ready to work, inspired and empowered.

And it wasn't long before she had the idea. She started on a project to find a tone, a sound, that would help prime the brain to remember, to maintain the precious data it had captured.

It would be a tool to help stave off Dementia.

13 - The Last Great Hero of Detroit

....

Humans landed on Detroit at the end of the 23rd century, aware that the planet's own sun would devour it within three hundred years.

Yes, they named it after THAT Detroit.

But humans often invent things out of necessity. Hundreds of years ago, we had an old adage about that but I forget it.

Novoth was the head of the sleep team, the leader, by default, on Detroit. And the whole thing was his idea.

Much like their beloved Earth, Detroit was alive. The planetary consciousness was strong and it WANTED to use its unique magics to save its children. It just needed to figure out how.

So, each night, their sleep team used the delicate machinery they had built to confer with the planetary mother to find a solution. A nighttime brainstorm, if you will.

And one morning, they had it.

With the help of the Planetary mother, the goddess of the ground, they would drive the planet like a ship to the next available star. It would take hundreds of years, two hundred and fifty, to be exact, but all of Detroit's seven million people would live, and thrive.

In order to make the trip, however, the entire population would have to burrow into the ground and stay there. The entire sleep team would then have jobs. They would need to carry out this trip, to save their people.

The planetary mother prepared to elevate and raise her champions. Each person, however, would need to first die to be reborn. They all willingly stepped forward and drank their own death from out of a tiny cup.

Chira rose first. The small, dark skinned woman had been given considerable abilities. Her perfect aim would help her navigate through obstacles. Her ability to communicate with the planet and shape its movements would let her drive it like a ship.

She was to be the pilot

Next to rise was Jekara. The powerful force blasts that now came from her eyes helped her not only see long distances but, with pinpoint precision, target and eliminate objects in her way. She would be the weapons system for an entire planet.

Then came Mondino. He was blessed with the ability to build and fix anything using his mastery of the ground and elements. He would maintain the ship they all lived on, fix it, keep it running smoothly.

And Viado would use his new powers of telepathy to connect them all together. He would be a living communication system across the planet they loved.

Novoth spent his additional time in death with the planetary mother to prepare him for his most special role. He rose with incredible regenerative abilities, the ability to grow to great heights, to block out pain.

He stood up and grew to his full fifty meter height. It is always important that a leader sacrifices. Novoth knew that, on a trip of this length, through space, beneath the ground, his people would have needs.

And he would be food.

14 - The Gospel of Johnny Fractal

A couple of years ago, Lida had invented an imaginary criminal mastermind, along with three other experts, set him on the world, and raked in almost three hundred billion dollars in profit...

the bulk of which was made from robbing mostly criminals.Because that's what Johnny Fractal was good at. And, in all honesty, it was what he was made for.

They split the money four ways and disappeared. Until one of them, a Cuban mercenary, killed the other two men. Lida had tried to bargain with him but he was a most expert killer and that was his most preferred means of communication .

She had given him her entire cut, in order to assuage him, but he continued to come. He was relentless, he was unstoppable.

And despite his experience, all over the world, he was as naive as all the other people Lida had encountered here.

How could a mercenary, a lawyer, a geneticist, and a simple computer hacker invent a fictional villain that would elude capture for twenty years and steal the GDP of a mid-sized South American country.

The correct answer is that they could not.

Lida powered up her tiny Raspberry pi PC, sliding it down her wrist. The man following her only knew her as Montana, her code name. To reinforce that, a couple of keystrokes on the smallish computer and the back of her coat began to shift and adjust.

Now, in white/silver against the black leather background, it said, in Blackletter type, "Montana."

She tried to remember what she had in the back of her mind about the man she knew as Nevada.

It wasn't much. But she had used all of it to give as good as she got. If he was out to kill her, she would kill him first

She found him in front of his wine cellar just two weeks later. The people stalking you are uniformly always surprised when you find them first. And he was no different. He tried to offer her money, but she could see him inching forward to the wall where he kept his weapons.

"I wouldn't do that." Montana whispered

He countered, "What are you even doing here? I didn't know I was going to be here. How are you finding me?

She could tell that the other was impressed. She watched him upgrade her, mentally.
Too late.

Nevada began to blink out, to fade, as though losing size in some not immediately visible dimension. He began to speak, "What the fuck," as he dissappeared in a ring of reddish orange flame, lifting up from the ground.

It was incredibly satisfying to Lida, even as she felt a tiny pain of regret.

Nevada had taught her so much, they all had. It wasn't really his fault he got greedy. All these humans are. But Lida considered now how the experience of building the greatest criminal of all time, from scratch, might help inform her next project.

She would create a god.

15 - Envelopes

....

Ok, you want a story? A story and I can go?

All right, once upon a time, there was this guy. I didn't know him personally.

But he was a husband, and a father. A good one.

That's what I hear.

He used to take his boy to the zoo. He used to laugh with the kid's mom. He wasn't one of those fathers that sit in front of the tv in their underwear, saying shush all the time. He was a dad. You know. A real dad.

I guess.

He joked a lot. He was funny. And he didn't give a shit who liked him.

But they did. People liked him

One day he gets it in his head to make things easier for his family.

And he goes to rob this bank.

And maybe he's by himself. Or had a guy. Or two. Or a hundred guys. Me, I like to think he was by himself. He didn't want anyone to get hurt, except maybe him if he did. Maybe he had some help on the inside. Maybe he didn't — maybe he had every thief in the whole town doing things, and maybe he didn't. I don't know

And neither did the cops. Or the feds. Or anybody else.

Because when they grabbed him up, he closed his mouth and that was the stopping point for all of it. The case began and ended with him. Because he closed his mouth.

Is this the story you wanted? Cause this is what I been told. It's a legend here in Charlestown. He closed his mouth. He said goodbye to his wife and to their boy and went to jail and he lived there for a little while

Until he died there. Because that's who cops bring. They bring badges and guns to your door and they let death in. And then they go home and beat their kids because fuck them. Right?

So then, it's possible that this is when the envelopes came. The thieves in this town who respect a shut mouth. Maybe they make sure the widow and her son got what they need. Because they sure as fuck don't have a dad. They got envelopes, though. And that's what they live on.

Because cops bring death. But thieves, they bring envelopes. With life inside. That's what they say, anyway.

And you, you think you can be a big man stopping the envelopes. That's how you want to make a name.

A town that lives on envelopes. Every time some car gets rolled or some bank gets tipped, the envelopes go out. Cause thieves take care of the families in this town that you fuck. And the more you fuck, the tighter the lips get and the more envelopes go out.

And that's life. In that white paper rectangle, Life. And you don't know shit about that. You do death. And you don't know shit about envelopes.

So that's your story. The end.

Can I go now?

16 - That Hole in the Wall

....

I don't obsess easily

For verification of this, you can check with my last three girlfriends. I was the cool boyfriend, above it all. I handled it. But there are times when you shouldn't "handle it". Like when Meg said she was pregnant. And I just "handled it" and she realized I wasn't the guy.

Not the guy you want to have a kid with, that's me. Nice to meet you.

That's where all this started, too. When Meg left, just a couple weeks later, she yelled. I didn't. She exploded. I didn't. Finally, she put her fist through the wall, right there, near the closet. I acted like an adult and I walked away. Which was good.

But I didn't match her intensity. I didn't care.

And that's bad. So I lost her. I don't want to manipulate you now or unnecessarily pull at your heartstrings telling you this, but, yes, she was the one. I loved her,

Maybe that's why I haven't patched up that hole yet. There was no real urgency. But, I realized earlier today, it was the 15th, and the apartment next door was being rented by the first, I'm sure.

Maybe their tolerance for a big old hole in the wall reminding them of my past breakups was lower than mine. Who could tell.

I'm not super handy but I can fix a hole. I picked up a patch, some spackle and paint and planned to do it really soon.

But then, that night, I saw a light coming from it - through the hole. It occurred to me that maybe new people were already moving in. I took a look through it and it didn't seem to look like the next door two bedroom. This hole should be in the living room area. But that's not what I saw.

It looked like a garden. Trees, plants, the sun shining. I thought maybe the Television next door was on. But I could smell it, too. And walking through the garden.

Well, that was Meg.

I pulled away from the wall. That was a sign. It's late, I'm tired, probably dreaming. Time for bed, right?

Except the next day, the light was still there. And the longer I looked the more it became obvious that it WAS Meg. Her mop of red hair, her fairy ears. In the Garden she was pregnant. It looked like it was near the end of her term.

I did the math and that wasn't possible. Even if this was a video of Meg and she hadn't gone through with the abortion, it would have only been a few months.

She was beautiful

By night time, the version of Meg in the Hole had given birth. A son. He was beautiful. And she looked happy. I called out and she couldn't hear me. I watched him grow into a handsome young man, Until one day, the hole was gone.

I hadn't cared enough to fix the hole.

But my son did.

17- Forgiveness

. . . .

Don took a longer than usual shower this morning and let the water wash over him in silence until it began to run cold. It was really a beautiful day and he had to admit he was incredibly excited.

He had marked this date in the calendar. August 25th was not just his anniversary. It was the birth of his son. It was the greatest trip they had ever taken. It was a day, year after year, when the world sort of aligned for them.

And they remembered.

Don pulled the black jeans on, covering the purplish bruises on his legs. He always bruised easily. But he didn't want to think about that today. Today was sort of a day of rest. But it was also an omen. It was a promise, in a way.

Jennifer met him by the pier at six. The sun was beginning to fall in the sky, and it advertised that fact with a dissolving palette of reds and oranges that looked for all the world as though they might have been unreproducible. She leaned into her husband and their lips met.

Kissing Jennifer always made Don feel like a good kisser. Her lips were round and responsive and pliant under his. It was a place he felt in control, and her lithe body under her sundress seemed committed to letting him feel that, curling into him like a cat might.

They didn't talk about David, off at Art School, making things work, a monthly stipend check from Dad helping to keep his world in order.

They didn't talk about a lot of things. They danced on the beach, like they did the night of their wedding, They held each other and made small talk, the smaller the better, about how skin felt and what the night air did to each of them.

They sat and had a late night picnic, which may sound to you like an adventure taken on by senior citizens unafraid of sand in their food, but for them, it was an excuse to let clothing fall away and hands wander and to recline in open spaces across a towel that was made for just this night, just this event.

Jennifer dropped the straps of her sundress and let her breasts take in and reflect the ongoing lightshow, like twin screens in the path of a projector, filling the night with ideas, things that were possible, ways that Don could feel close to her once again, something they both may have needed desperately.

They used up the night and parted at light.

This August 25th was hopeful. It was a day of forgiveness that suggested that, one day, there would be more. Like every year, it was the day when Jennifer abandoned her brutal pursuit of justice, haunting and haranguing him, and forgave him for one day out of respect for all the good they had before he killed her and left her body to wash away in the receding tide.

18- The Last Witch Trial

....

To Ahya Abdul-Aziz James Junkung Jammeh, The Gambia was full of witches and someone needed to stop them.

And so, in 1996, the people, by an overwhelming percentage, agreed and helped him to take over the government and become the second president of the Gambia specifically to do just that.

His first official act was to gather up the suspected witches. So they came for Dima.

Dima Jawara was the cousin of Dawda Jawara, the man that Jammeh had taken the throne from. Dima was a fisherman who lived near the border of Senegal. A simple man, he was also a wise one, one who knew things...

But certainly no witch.

Had Jammeh been a person interested in other people, however, which he was not, he might have noticed that his chief of staff, Colonel Nicolas Ambawe was.

Ambawe was older, near seventy-years old. He had lived long enough to despise Jammeh for his cruelty and his burgeoning dictatorship.

By the time Jammeh was raised to power, the Colonel's magicks had rendered him thin and sickly. The sicker Jammeh got, though, the more he had Jawara tortured, hoping to release the spell.

When Ambawe finally visited Jawara in prison, it was a remorseful, penitent version of himself. He told Jawara that he would confess that he himself was the witch and see to it Jawara was freed immediately.

But DIma grabbed his outreached hand and held it. He told the older man that he couldn't do that. Jammeh must die and only a powerful witch like him could do it. He was willing to be tortured for that future. Ambawe walked away with a newfound purpose. Every morning he used his magic to damage the president even more - to hurt him.

As Jammeh became more sick, he became more cruel. He ordered Dima's family killed, brutally. He had his daughter's severed head placed in his cell.

Dima loved his family and was crushed beyond all consolation. But he still insisted that HE was the witch, letting the Colonel drive the president's health further to the ground.

Jammeh lost the use of his legs from the magics used by Ambawe. This made him even angrier. Blaming Dima, he had his men charge into his cell and break each of the prisoner's legs to shards. And still he insisted he was the witch. And Jammeh insisted that he release him from the curse or the torture would continue.

Dima's mind was shattering from the abuse. But he didn't give in. Not even when Jammeh shot his own Colonel Ambawe in front of him and made Dima eat his remains.

Now, no one knows exactly how witches are made. It's often speculated that they learn the ways of power because they are broken by other powers and must, despite all of it, rise.

Whatever this recipe was, Jammeh had inadvertently replicated it in his treatment of Dima.

Some believe he realized that as the blood drained from his body and he fell dead.

19- Awake

Originally, Degan Montroy articulated in his testimony, it was a curse. A curse muttered at him by an older foreign woman when he woke her up unceremoniously on the train. He could trace it back to that night. But it wasn't hard. She scowled at him and then touched his arms and said:

"Awake"

And he was. The court listened as Montroy testified that he would never again sleep after this. Not even for a minute. He would never rest his eyes. He would never drift away. He was just, constantly, without exception, every night, awake. No one believed it, of course. Degan had to admit he wouldn't have believed it either.

But the defense had assembled reams of documentation speaking to Montroy's unique condition. Not one of the doctors believed it was a curse, but none of them could deny the reality of what was happening.

That Degan montroy could never go to sleep.

It was hard to buy. He looked alert, conscious, even tidy. He was soft spoken and intelligent. Psychiatrists from all over the country had spent days at a time with him trying to prove his conditions had driven him mad.

But it hadn't He looked healthier than you or I. He was wearing a shirt he had spun himself one night, in place of sleep. It was really quite beautiful. He had used his extra time to learn three additional languages. His skin looked like the skin of a man who had learned to cook a rarified menu of delicious yet extremely healthy food,

And his shoes were buffed and shined every morning.

The defense had nothing. There was a simple and easy trail to each victim, murdered in their sleep by this man. He didn't even bother denying it. In the end, the only thing extending the sentencing was his assertion that he would tell the authorities WHY he did it in exchange for suitable accommodations.

He wanted a comfortable room, no bed, free access to media, books and films,. He wanted his own kitchen and groceries sufficient to cook.

The DA caved almost immediately. Two bodies remained to be found and his bosses were on him to make sense of these motiveless crimes.

The truth was that he was perfectly sane. He was unerringly sane. His problem may have been he was too sane.

When you watch someone sleep for a night or two they seem adorable - vulnerable. You want to take care of them. They're like a baby, really. Helpless.

But what if that baby never grew up? And you had to be wide awake as they slept for a full third of the day, every day. They start to seem useless, lazy, pointless...

...Weak.

They start to make you angry. So unable to take care of themselves for a giant gap in their lives, dull, boring, trivial, nonsensical. They looked breakable, like the least little thing could snap them in half like a dried twig.

And, Degan Montroy discovered, it could.

20 - Butterfly

....

"Sit, kid. Sit, you're making me fucking nervous."

"Look, Nothing bad happened here tonight. Barely nothing illegal
happened. You came right up against illegal like a butterfly, a fucking
butterfly. You rubbed illegal's belly. And I know that you got 2k in your
pocket from it."

"Got to feel a little good."

"And that's yours. Nobody is going to take that away. You earned it and
that's good. But think about it. You didn't lift your arm for that money.
You didn't raise your hand. You didn't open your mouth, you didn't write
a number, clock in, check out, call someone, text anyone. Wave your dick,
nothing."

"You shut your fucking mouth and you earned $2,000."

"Look, I don't know you, Richard. I don't know how you live. I know me,
and if I had 2k in my pocket for nothing, I'd be looking to do nothing a little
more regularly. I'd be looking to brush up like a butterfly more often, right
up to that line. Even if I didn't want to cross that line. I'd be like, Bring me
to that line. Let me get right up on that line and fucking earn."

"I'd get friendly with that line, because it's a beautiful straight line that
doesn't ask much out of you. And if every time you rub your ass up against
it, you walk away two k heavier, is that really so bad?"

"

So this is you, Rich. you nod, you look, you keep your mouth shut. You snake your body right up against that line like a butterfly, and you can have that every week. That's a lot of money, man, for doing nothing. It's a lot of money. It's 'buy a house when you get a little older' money if you plan right. If you're smart, and I can see that you are smart as fuck."

"I know this isn't how you see yourself and believe it or not, I can relate to that. There's lots of shit I wanted to be, trust me on that. But I also know that people like us got expenses and if we gotta be honest, people like us don't see the point of the police coming down on some reasonable trade between reasonable people. Do I have us understood well? Tell me I understand people like us, Richard."

"Go Home, Rich. Think about it. Like a butterfly. Right up against it. And then,

Poof."

The older man waved his hands slowly, like he was doing a belly dance.

The kid looked back over his shoulder as he walked out. He was considering all the wrong things.

And that's good. Elian knew what to do to get people to want to see his point. He'd had thousands of years by now, to learn how to make his words sail home, to convince them that he was a criminal, a thief, a drug dealer, a con man, anything but what he really was.

Because the best souls came unexpectedly.

21 - This Charlie Here

....

I'm an old woman now, so I guess it no longer matters. But you're the kind of person who loves adventure. You probably have some idea why I'm doing this. And why I'm leaving this note.

First of all, I apologize if I'm not the person you thought I was. Please be comforted by the fact that I'm not the person I thought I was, either and that's probably a bit more fucked, really.

I don't really have many of the memories I had before the accident. You know that. I'll tell you what I do know.

I was hit by a car in Ocean City, New Jersey on April 14th, 2019. I was wearing a dirty Atlantic City T-shirt, a pair of jeans, carrying no identification, and had no money or effects, except for a one year sobriety chip in my front pocket, in that little hidden area.

Once I woke up, it took them over a month to discover who I was and get me sent back to a hospital in Chicago, where I eventually recovered in every way except for the maddening gaps in my memories.

That was twenty-five year old Charlie. Today, at sixty, sitting here in my primary home in Victory City, surrounded by opulence, dressed in a three-thousand-dollar Verikund Maple Leaf Dress from Dior, I still have questions for that Charlie.

Like where were my clothes? Where was my purse? Why was I so obviously sickly?

And why did I have a sobriety chip when I've been a tea-totaler my whole life?

Sean, you've tried to explain some of this to me at first. But, as I discovered from your late night confession yesterday, it was mostly lies.

So, no, I couldn't really tell you anything.

I guess I don't really belong in this universe. It's not my original one. But it's where my body accidentally transported me when I was hit by that car. A body that is only aging because I think I age. A body that is falling apart because I think I'm human.

And humans fall apart. Stop me if I misunderstood.

In this universe, I'm a wealthy woman. I can have anything I want. And, apparently, I've taken advantage of that. I own seventeen cars and three motorcycles. As far as I know, I've never been on a motorcycle. And I'm not one hundred percent sure I can drive.

In this universe, You are my partner. We traveled here together. I don't know what happened to the Sean in my Universe, if there ever was one. But you've tried to keep me safe, to protect me from myself. You said that the only reason I would have lost my memory is if those memories were dangerous to me.

Let's find out.

Sean, I don't know much. And I'm sorry if I'm taking all this worse than you had hoped. But I'm going home. If you really love me, maybe you'll find me, And we can share one more adventure.

22 - Every Wound In The World

By the beginning of the twenty-first century, it became clear that if you wanted something done right, do it yourself, but if you wanted something done BIG, get a shitload of crazy people to do it with you.

These were the kinds of observations Aurelius made all the time. And he'd been making them since the eleven hundreds when he was just a kid, trying to extend his life. Hell, he had practically invented the discipline of Alchemy. Then neuromancy, psychology, medicine. Just to live one more day.

But, as the adage above indicated, he needed to go bigger if he intended to really live forever, or at least as long as he needed to. He had harnessed order and purpose, function, the control that comes from Knowledge. It only made sense for him to harness the other side of that coin.

To put a leash around chaos.

Then, in 1618, something interesting happened. A series of minor upheavals across Europe created the conditions for a war that spread across all the nations of the continent. We know it now as the thirty years war. But at the time, it just seemed like an entire generation of unending confusing chaos.

And it generated massive chaotic energy.

Aurelius was able to tap that energy and use it to power his magicks and continue to stay vibrant and young. But it was a drawn out war, spread all over, so the energy was dissipated, hard to capture. And it hurt his heart that so many were killed, maimed, or hurt by this mass act of chaos.

So, in the 18th century he founded the Secret order of Occult Chaoticians. Their goal was to create chaotic events across the world that could feed into the Occult Energy that Aurelius needed. But, hopefully, without the death and destruction of a war.

And they created, throughout the years, enough chaos to keep him alive for centuries. Once they caused an event that switched every man on earth into a woman, and every woman into a man.

That was worth centuries of life.

One day, Aurelius stood in front of the Kha Plate - the device that had brought order to his life, showed him his future, and made it possible for him to work to live- to reach it.

The myth was that the Ka Plate was left behind by a hidden race of travelers. It showed timelines, futures, even different dimensions and worlds.

Something dawned on him.

This very thing that had brought perfect order to Aurleius' life - what kind of chaos would it bring to the lives of other people?

What if he tasked his chaoticians with placing these all over, in unexpected places. In windows, behind walls, doorways, the holes in trees, cabinets, and more. What kinds of chaos could these tiny viewports to other realities create?

Like cuts - open sores all over.

Aurelius would argue later that it was just an uninformed idea...

...His part in creating every wound in the world.

23 - The Shittiest Vampire

....

"Gerrold, no, this does not work for me." Vance turned his head and stared at the other Vampire.

He responded with a shaky voice. "No, I'm a bad 17 year old. I mean, I was a bad 17 year old when I was a 17 year old, that's how I ended up getting bit in the first place. It's been 200 years, now. Really, I promise you I am no better at all this shit now"

He moved his hands around as though he were spreading out imaginary puzzle pieces, Vance was a bad hand talker.

"Dude." Gerold was just a bad talker.

"Seriously. Why can't you do this? You're believable. Here, say something. I'll believe it."

"I barely talk. You're the only one I talk to."

"Dude. Do you know what teenagers did when I was a teenager? Do you know what was in? Masturbating in the outhouse and dying of dysentary. This all came back to lack of indoor plumbing. Seriously, that is the entire picture of my 18th century teenage experience. Then I died for real. "

"You have to take care of it, then." Gerrold was ready to wash his hands of the whole thing. He was bigger and older and even talking to Vance was exhausting. "Eat her."

Vance backed up a bit.

"Fuck. No, we can't eat her now. I don't really eat people who give me a ride home. It's the tiniest, teensiest shred of a moral code I can cling to as a fucking vampire. Don't take that away from me.

Gerrold advanced, "Just Fix it."

The larger Vampire disappeared in the night, as they do sometimes. He was Viaje and honestly much meaner than Vance had thought. He could have ripped out Vance's throat with a movement. And Vance was sure he would. Without a distraction.

Vance looked around and then down at the girl folded up in the back seat. He opened her wallet with one hand and read her driver's license. "And who names their kids Helen anymore? Isn't that an ancient Greek name?" He sounded a little sad as he continued. "I don't know, Helen, you were in the wrong fucking place and wrong time tonight. You could have gotten eaten."

Her voice came the the darkness of the seat cushions, "I liked the part about masturbating in an outhouse and dying of Dysentary."

"All true. People forget how bad it smelled two hundred years ago, Helen. Don't ever be nostalgic for the past." He fished through her purse and found the keys, starting the car up.

"Why did you save me?" she asked quietly.

"I don't know, Helen. Why did you distract that psychopath at the bar and save me?" Vance started the car and realized he was a terrible driver. He could man the hell out of a horse and carriage, though.

"Because I have no sense of self-preservation?" She sat up as the car began to move.

"Meh, let's figure it out tomorrow."

And they did.

24 - The Church of the Liberator

I wonder how many times, in the history of police work, tracking down a missing cat is the solution to a bigger case. You have to think it's happened more than once.

In this case, it was that Raynard Parker thing. The part about the cat probably didn't make it to the news. I suspect the police don't want the entire thing to become common knowledge. What would happen if it did?

I have no idea. But it terrifies me.

Reynard led the Church of the Liberator, and was a standard issue cult leader. You can check the boxes. He wore his brown hair long and was convinced that he was the incarnation of Jesus. He isolated and insulated his followers from mainstream media. And he took wives, many of them, from the women and young girls in the congregation.

New York state authorities had tried to pinpoint their compound near the Hudson at Bear Mountain Bridge for almost a year. They couldn't locate the main facility - where most of the church members lived. But they kept looking.

Why do the authorities care about these things, you probably ask?

There is a historical precedent for these kinds of cults becoming more dangerous as time wears on. Think of it as Michael Jackson / R Kelly Syndrome. The longer people let them get away with stuff the weirder that shit got.

Until, you know.

Raynard had sent his manifesto to the local papers and that, in itself, was a huge wakeup call. They published it on page two. It talked about how he was made invulnerable by blood magic, the willing gift of his member's lives, each making him stronger. This was frightening and caused the state police to step up their search.

On page 30 of that same paper, however, was the story that broke the case. It was about Samael, the cat owned by Maggie Devers, the local Diner operator. Samael had disappeared forcing her to put out a one hundred dollar reward for information to Animal control leading to his safe return.

But animal control found Samael from the GPS tracker in his tiny collar, in the Church of the Liberator's sub basement, happily licking away at the sea of blood made by the three hundred or so church members who had opened their veins with tiny ceremonial knives just minutes before.

They called the police and they stormed the Liberation compound almost immediately. There were heavy casualties on both sides, but no one from the Church survived.

Who knows what would happen if the footage from the compound got out on the internet and people could see Reynard in that final fight with the police. Would people think that it was altered to show him, barechested, his wild hair whipping around behind him in the wind, feet lifting off the ground, with his eyes lit with the fires stoked by the hundreds of fresh corpses below him and their willing gift of a blood magic that actually worked?

25 - Apeworld - World of Apes

....

The most fucked-up beginning of an apocalypse, hands down, has to go to the 2064 Worldwide Ape Uprising.

This is more Jurassic Park than Jurassic Park. And I say that to mean that this was preventable. This was really preventable. But we humans, we don't always pay the most attention to stuff.

Backing up a little to 2060, some group of poorly-paid scientists discover that Chimpanzees and Gorillas have racial memories. Everyone is focused on the fact that this means we humans probably do, too. We can pass memories and skills around that are built within the community.

Now, everyone is excited. That's cool. And then most people forget about it. Except for this LA Comic who does a whole routine around the old movie, "Rise of the Planet of the Apes," Which goes viral all over TikTok.

Here's where the story kind of gets interesting.

Sorry about the previous few paragraphs.

The newfound popularity of chimps and Apes causes Disney to open an exhibit called, unironically "Apeworld - the World of Apes." Obviously tantalized by the narrative redundancy of the title, people swarm it in droves yelling "take my money." Disney does.

Now, here's the thing. Apeworld - World of Apes used real chimps and gorillas. It turned out to be cheaper than the Animatronic ones. There is a social commentary there, but we'll keep moving.

But, to keep them doing what their Disney overlords wanted them to do, they hired paid actors to lead them.

These actors wore state-of-the-art hyper realistic Ape Suits so real that the Apes themselves could not tell they weren't Chimps, Gorillas, etc. They even smelled like it. The suits took hours to take off and put on so they were made as comfortable as possible.

Now, taking advantage of the way that Apes learn, all these actors had to do was do what they were instructed to do and the apes around them would learn. Many of these up-and-coming performers were method actors. They chose to just LIVE there, with the Apes, in costume, 24/7.

You can probably see this coming.

The Apes started to learn. They didn't just learn what they were supposed to do, they learned what the actors did on their time off, just hanging out. They learned how to talk. They learned how to read. They learned how to drive a car, how to make Italian food, how to do all these things.

And when the actors went on strike, they learned that, too.

They passed this knowledge on, racially, to the ether, where Apes all over the world began to pick up skills, rise up...

And go on strike.

Apes stormed cities all over the world, eating at no-pets-allowed cafes, applying for jobs at Lockheed International, getting state IDs and maxing out LINK cards with fresh fruit. They were everywhere.

We remember this tale of human stupidity today as we head to the polls. One species dropped the ball while the other one picked it up.

So, Vote Ape.

26 - Movers

....

Ke said, "so, what's in the box?" She looked over at the man in the blue suit and nondescript face, "murder weapon? One of those ugly dolls? I had one, too. I didn't want anyone to know, either."

The man became clearly agitated, "Does she have to be here?"

Roman sighed, "She's one of those people who can be anywhere she wants to be."

"Who's this guy?" Ke returned fire.

Roman looked him up and down, "Oh, he wants me to call him 'K' which means his name is something embarrassing for a grownup, like 'Kevin'"

Kevin blurted out, "it's not Kevin..."

Roman continued, "And he wants me to make this gone. So we, for our part, don't want to know what's in it."

Ke offered, "sounds convenient"

Roman huffed. "Are you sure you never want to see this box or the contents of this box again? I will not know where this box is or have it in my ability to retrieve it. Understood?"

Kevin reiterated, "Understood. I read the contract." The box seemed to suck into itself, but its size remained constant, almost like it was losing size only in a dimension that wasn't immediately obvious. In a second, it was gone, its absence accompanied by a tiny pop of inrushing air.

Kevin looked up, less impressed than Roman imagined he would be."I could almost see where that went. Almost."

Roman's phone dinged in his pocket, "And that's your payment, going through. I appreciate it. " Roman wiped his hands off on a small towel and threw it over his shoulder, looking more like a mechanic than ever. "Is that a wand, Kevin?."

"For the love of,,," Kevin pulled a long stick out from his coat jacket. "My name isn't Kevin. Seriously, shit," The wand faded away. "Give that back"

Roman continued. "Nope. But here's a lesson. In 2013, Alex Schlegel, a grad student in the department of psychological and brain sciences at Dartmouth searched for the seat of imagination in your brain. Apparently there is a place in your brain, a neural network that coordinates activity across several regions of the brain, consciously manipulating ideas and images, concepts, etc. If you tried to imagine a Bull with the head of a bee, this is the part of your brain that would invent that image. And the part you use to do what we do. Your mental workspace. I just reached in and removed it from your brain."

"You brain damaged me."

"I could make the case you were brain damaged when you walked in here," Ke shot back.

"Kevin," Roman's fingers snapped, "Focus. Stop looking at your hand."

Kevin tried to wipe away the markings on his hand."You moved a tattoo onto me. How did you do that?"

"Do not look at it. Without a mental workspace to visualize. It will get stuck in your head and you'll disappear"

"Fuck." Kevin looked down and disappeared. Ke paused.

"There was a certain amount of inevitability to that. "

27 - The Battle With the Blur

··

This was the first time Andrew had ever been in a room with the blur long enough to hear why. But first, Andrew had to talk.

So he did.

It started because of a grade school prom. He woke up waiting for that night, when he and Amy would finally show the whole school they were together. She was out of his league. She was beautiful, funny, and had the most amazing voice. She was perfect. But she was going to prom with him.

At school. He entered in the back, near the football field, close to his locker. It was quieter back there. And that's when he saw it.

He watched the Blur kill sixteen-year-old Amy Wilkes right in front of his eyes.

Andrew ran up to the scene but he was too late. He tried to grab the blur who turned and looked at him.

With his own face.

Suddenly, Andrew found himself somewhere else. A different version of the world he knew. It looked so similar. But there were subtle changes. The school team was called the Cobras, not the Hawks. There was more. Amy's body had traveled with him. He dragged it away and left it in the forest behind the school. He couldn't explain this. He found home in this alternate dimension and fit right in. In his room, taped to the mirror, was the ruby. The note attached called it "Tau Kharada." It was beautiful. He picked it up and thought to himself.

He needed to find Amy.

Suddenly he was back at the school. It was night and everything looked different. Alien, foreign. He turned just in time to see the Blur killing twenty-five-year-old English Teacher Amy Wilkes. He rushed up to stop him and suddenly he and the body were back home.

In the dimension he just left.

He looked down at this Amy's body. He would have to place it with the last one.

Within the next few months, he had collected over twenty versions of Amy Wilkes, at various ages, from various locations, each killed brutally by the blurry man with his face.

Andrew was tired and his heart was broken.

When the police came for him, he offered no resistance.

Which is how Andrew Jellique found himself sitting in a jail cell, awaiting execution, with a blurry version of himself leaning against the sink asking him questions.

The Blur was older than he was, more confident. But his eyes were wild, as though he had no control over them.

He told Andrew about how he had found the ruby and had tried to give it to Amy as a gift. She turned it down and canceled their prom date. The ruby split him into two parts, one that did it and the other who did not.

Andrew looked past him in the mirror and say that his face was blurry, too

And would be until he fixed it.

He reached out to the other Andrew. And brought him home.

28 - The Interview

....

"Is it ok if we talk?" a strange man slid into the Diner booth across from Jeron, who searched his face for recognition.

"Do I know you?" Jeron was a quiet, sad woman. She didn't have many friends at this time in her life.

"You've been talking about killing me for months now. One sec." The older man ordered a piece of pie before returning his attention back to the man across from him.

"I don't know what you think you heard, but..."

"Ever since Julian died, you think about killing God every night."

Jeron sat there confused for a minute. How could he have known that? He asked, "So you're God?"

"For now, yes." the man stared right through Jeron.

"What does that mean," Jeron asked.

God took a bite of pie, thanking the waitress. "It means I'm the most recent one with the job. But consider this a job interview."

"To be God?." Jeron was very confused.

"Do you want to be?"

Jeron had the answer available. "I want God to be SOMEONE good"

"And you think he's not? That I'm not?"

"My son." Jeron sullenly pulled a picture of the boy from her wallet.

"I see." The man pulled out a drawing of an ape. "This was mine." Jerrod held the drawing. It seemed to move. "I took this job about three million years ago. I was australopithecus but I make some adjustments when I talk to humans. Is the coffee good here?"

"It's ok." Jerron leaned in, "Your son died?"

"All my children died. To add insult to injury, my people died out before we got to be you people."

"So why did you want this job?"

"Because SOMEONE good had to do it."

"How can you call yourself good...?"

"Are you a chess person?"

Jerron wasn't. But she liked to think she could learn. "I could learn. "

"Don't bother, but let me ask you this. Do you think you could play a chess game - even if you controlled both sides and every move - could you play it in such a way that every piece got what they wanted and no one was ever hurt?"

"If you controlled both sides?" Jerron thought. She knew what the answer was supposed to be. How could both queens, for example, have what they wanted?

"So there is no Satan? "

"There doesn't have to be. You could invent him if you want. I highly recommend it. It makes the time go much faster. But every piece on that board. They want something. And sometimes you can make a game where they all win.

Could you do better?"

Jerron imagined that maybe she could.

"How do I apply for the job?"

"There is no application. You're hired if you want it."

"How do I accept the Job?"

The stranger stood up to leave. "Just do the first thing. In your heart.

Always do what's in your heart."

The Waitress arrived a few minutes later with a piece of pie for Julian..

29 - Made to Win

....

Kurt would hum a little bit in the morning on his way to work.

He would take the 17 bus Down Yale to the Victory City boatyard humming.

Then he'd clock in, humming a bit. Then he'd shine some boats.

He'd be humming when he did that, too.

Kurt enjoyed what he did.. He liked the lack of pressure. He liked his life simple. He had one friend, Mike, and he liked him. The two of them used to meet up every Thursday after work and drink a little bit.

Friday was a work day.

So when Mike saw that Kurt stopped going to work, and didn't show up two Thursdays in a row, he went to his apartment to see him.

Then he found the video.

Mike had a key and let himself in. He heard the video from the other room. It was Kurt speaking. He started it over at the beginning.

"Hi, Mike. I'm assuming this is you. I'm leaving this video to explain what's been going on with me. You should probably sit down."

Mike sat on Kurt's overstuffed green couch.

"Six days ago, I fell in the shower. I scraped my arm and the skin came off from my wrist to my elbow. When I tried to clean it and close the wound, getting ready to go see a doctor, I saw this."

On the video, he lifted his arm. Mike squinted to see. You couldn't tell, right away, what was going on. It looked like blue and silver chrome, with a fine web of wires throughout. He continued,

"Maybe you can see, maybe not. It's a network of wires and electronics. I was confused, since I had never had anything like that implanted in me. But there it was. Later that day, I removed the skin from my chest to investigate more closely what was going on."

He lifted his shirt. Now there was no doubt. Mike took a step back. In the video, Kurt's entire chest had had the skin pulled off. And where you would expect to see muscle, blood, bone, instead was a complex skein of wiring and futuristic looking machine parts. There was a clearly computerized heart beating alongside 4 hydraulic pumping lungs. He had to admit, it was good work. It looked like the beautiful engineering of a competent robotics engineer, way ahead of his time.

"I want to be clear that I don't have any memory of any of this. As a machine, I had to have been made for something - some purpose. And I'm going to find out. Goodbye, Mike."

Mike sat staring as the video looped. The Kurt on the screen was intentional, directed, not content to just hum and live his little life. Now that he knew he was a machine, he needed to DO something. To BE something. To succeed.

Mike fingered the toolkit in his pocket and nodded.

He thought about Kara, the grocery store cashier, and how she always seemed so happy.

30 -Kuebiko

Hanzo jumped from the sheer rock face to the far outcropping about one hundred meters above the swirling Jinto passage, in its most restricted spot, water breakers foaming white against the cool blue of the speeding water. He grabbed on to the smallest nub in the far wall with his rubber reinforced gloves and slowly pulled his body over the top to stand on the craggy plateau made by the high altitude wind assailing the rocks for centuries.

He felt alive.

Hanzo was never happier than at times like now, when his search for knowledge brought him to strange and exotic parts of the world, pulling him inexorably toward the places where the seats of wisdom lay. Each of these fonts of pure wisdom were sedentary, locked, needing nothing, wanting nothing, purely inspired and enlightened to be, just be. As the student, he knew he had to travel to reach them, and each time he became a little better at it.

Hanzo was strong, lithe, with muscles up and down his abdomen and chest, He was built to travel, to find, to discover. And his arms and legs were honed by climbing, running, searching. He had once found a box containing secret knowledge, the Marigana, made from the entire core of a tree, carved in one piece, requiring a master keysmith to open, and from it he had learned so much.

Today, his goal was to reach the Keubiko, a legendary font of pure wisdom, who was rumored to hold the last piece of the puzzle he had gleaned from the Marigana.

Hanzo felt alive, felt invigorated to learn. He was covered in sweat but close.

On top of the rocky plateau, as he moved forward, there was an expanse of grass that had no earthly right to be there. As Hanzo kept walking, the grass became taller, wilder. He found himself in the center of a winding web of weeds that opened into a clearing that looked, for all the world, like an open cornfield.

Kuebiko stood in the midst of the field, an unmoving scarecrow. As Hanzo approached, he whispered the one word he needed.

Hanzo left him gratefully, stepping into an open clearing beyond, surrounded by a small blue brook.

Hanzo was not stupid. He realized at some point that this would happen. He moved forward to the clearing with a weariness in his legs. It wasn't a physical weariness, but more a lack of desire on the part of his appendages to move, to seek anymore. He had always known that one day he would evolve from being the petitioner, the student, vigorously seeking knowledge, to the teacher, the sedentary source of knowledge that had no will to explore, no wants, no needs, perfectly enlightened.

It took all his strength to move the few feet needed for him to occupy the quiet spot amidst the clearing, the simple bubbling of the brook rising in his ears as the perfect soundtrack to the rest of his days.

31 - Rogue Won

....

"I always had this feeling that when Anakin went from being good to bad in minutes, that something was weird. It felt wrong. Ok, hear me out, he was protecting the younglings and training them, and then, a little bit later, he just, killed them all. Like, what if, I know this sounds crazy. What if he didn't kill them. Instead, he made it look like he killed them then he sort of moved them all to a secret location and trained them. And now there is this like army of new Jedi waiting to attack and no one will ever know? Is that something that you think is like, possible? Could that have happened?"

Death shifted uncomfortably in his seat on the bed next to Reggie. He had started to zone out a bit. "Huh? Oh, is that your question?"

"Yes. Is that possible, do you think?"

"Well, I'm not really much of a Star Trek guy, really…"

Reggie sat up straighter, "It's Star Wars, actually."

"Do you have a real question you want to ask, about life or your place in it, or meaning, or…" For centuries, Death had been giving humans a chance to ask a single question before death, about anything. In that time, he'd fielded some great questions. But also, there had been moments like this.

Reggie looked at him with determination, "Honestly, most of the questions I really could ask were answered by Rogue One."

"I don't know what that is," Death responded sullenly.

"Oh, it's an amazing movie." Reggie pulled himself from bed and went to grab a DVD from his collection.

"That's not necessary."

"It totally is. It's a good introduction to the Star Wars universe, and it feeds directly into Episode 3."

Death stood up, "Episode 3?"

Reggie looked excited to tell someone. He was eighty four years old and the last visit he had had was a few weeks ago. From a son completely uninterested in great cinema. Reggie was still vibrant, though. His tight curl of black hair above his onyx black skin had just started to grey. And despite a little pause when getting in and out of bed, he was sprightly and alive. "A New Hope. It's the very first Star Wars movie that ever came out."

"And Rogue one happens right before it?"

"Yes, and it's a perfect movie."

Death pulled the chair toward him and slid into it. And then they watched the entire thing together. "You still haven't told me your question," Death looked down now at Reggie, afterward.

Reggie responded with concern in his eyes. "Are you ok?" all of this seems... Hard."

Death mentally took a step back. "Yeah. It is." He paused. "Do YOU need some more time, Reggie?"

"No. I'm old. You do your job. But you got to admit, that movie was good."

Death put his hand on Reggie's shoulder and could feel the kindness in him wash over him as he left. He whispered.

"No. It was great."

32 - Generation Two

Morale had never been high on the UEF Jemison, despite it being the flagship, and the most expensive ship ever designed, in the United Earth Fleet.

Right before the ship had launched, a version of that same ship appeared from about one hundred years in the future. It carried over two hundred descendants of the original thirty eight crew complement and massive structural damage.

And, in its computer systems, a record of what had happened.

The ship had been through a war, and paid an exorbitant price for it. Over half of the original crew were killed or maimed.

Apparently, The Jemison had come in contact with an alien race of people on a distant asteroid. It landed, to share supplies and trade when these people, the Nalkin, were attacked by a warlike race - a race of giant evolved Beetles.

The people on the Jemison had a choice. To stay and fight for their new friends or to leave in a ship that was much faster than those employed by the Beetles.

They stayed. And they fought. It took seven years but they were finally able to turn the tide and save the Nalkin. They left that tiny asteroid with supplies, an entire hold full of corpses, and a friendship with a people that would have died out entirely without them.

The next ninety plus years were fairly uneventful, with the ship failing at its ultimate goal of finding a new home for humanity. So when they encountered a wormhole with a trajectory that led back to earth, they entered it, arriving less than a year before they left.

The United Earth fleet had decisions to make. To change history and keep the Jemison from launching or to save the Nalkin and launch on schedule. After much internal debate it was decided to launch as anticipated. It was hard to argue against the survival of an entire race of people. And all thirty eight people on board agreed, even knowing what they did, that they would go.

So there wasn't much of a chance that morale would improve anytime soon. The crew, however, had bonded over their sacrifice and were committed to each other. If it was their job to be heroes, they would be.

They began to train every day for the eventual battle. They worked, they worked out. They became exemplary fighters.

Which is why the rest of this story is so ironic.

On the anniversary of their sixth year, a group of three aliens appeared on the bridge.

Of them, the taller woman blinked, her eyelids moving fluidly from side to side. She told them that they were the Raza, a race of aliens who could travel in time and space. She told them that their ship's records had been fabricated. There was no Nalkin, no race, no war. But now the Raza knew what kind of people they were.

They knew what they would do to help others.

So she invited them to a bigger conversation.

33 - Stateless

....

It started when scientists invented a new state of matter

If you only finished high school science, you may think there are only three states of matter, liquid, solid, and gas. If you went to college for a year or to, you know Plasma is another state. If you went further, you may be familiar with quantum condensates, and others.

Quark-Gluon Plasmas, degenerate matter, etc.

Recently it had been discovered that the small scale teleporters we had inherited as a people from alien friends used Photonic Matter, a state of matter where photons pretended to have mass for a while.

Altogether, twenty two states of matter had been discovered, Rydberg Polaronic matter that contained atoms within atoms.

And humans had just discovered the twenty third. Feynman-Distillate matter was a kind that had some very unusual qualities. It was gaseous and permeable in the first three dimensions but completely solid and superdense in the fourth. So it actually blocked ambient interaction with fourth dimensional models completely.

And that's what the box on the ambassador's desk was made from. The box that contained a rat suspended in air. The box had been applied while the rat was leaping from one place to another. And when it solidified, time inside stopped completely.

And the rat was frozen.

Theo sat staring at the rat, considering what a morbid thing that the Ambassador could have on his desk. Since the invention of the twenty-third state of matter, though, he knew that many people had taken to placing garish displays like this in public. This one was ironic, though.

The ambassador entered, sullen. "I'm sorry to have kept you."

Theo was not keenly aware of the presence of the secret service men behind him. He wasn't crazy about this job, for sure.

"I take it the appeal was denied," the ambassador began to collect papers from his desk. He pulled the Karakistani flag down from its perch on the wall and folded it gently.

Theo tried to sound casual, "Yes, sir."

And I am to accompany you to my country to serve my sentence with them?

Theo took a deep breath and repeated, "Yes, sir."

The Ambassador looked into Theo's face and saw him for what he was - a low level bureaucrat. He reached into the drawer, still holding Theo's gaze, and pulled a gun, shooting both men behind him before turning it on himself and firing, from beneath his chin, sending blood and brain matter spraying fountain-like, into the room.

Theo jumped, surprised at how long it had taken him. He didn't understand what had just happened. To the ambassador, and the rest of Karakistan, the sentence would be nothing. Being behind the FD wall would just feel like waking up 200 years in the future. No time would have passed. He looked down at the encased rat on the man's desk. It was spattered with specks of blood covering the clear block face of the box, over his forever unseeing eyes.

People swarmed in.

34 - That Endless Buffet

....

The coffee mug had the picture of a black cat on it and the logo for Samael's Diner. Miguel and his friends had each stolen one at 1am right after prom, sitting in the diner, laughing, planning how they would always be friends and never lose touch for the rest of their lives, knowing realistically, that it had taken no small miracle of planning, even now, to get them all together that night.

And it would only get harder.

They wouldn't have guessed, however, that Miguel would be the last one there, sitting in that booth, twenty years later, with a notepad full of math equations that didn't add up.

The Diner was named after Samael, Maggie's cat. Maggie used to always joke that he was the actual owner. And Miguel had been there at least once a week for his whole life. Over the last few weeks, it had been an almost religious experience, though.

The Hudson Valley Diner here was famous for a few things, besides the cat. One of its biggest draws was, every weekend, the all-you-can-eat breakfast buffet. For legal reasons, pointing to how communities deal with issues around obesity, buffets like this were now called "Endless."

Miguel had no idea how that was any better, but he did think that "Endless Buffet" sounded like a romance novel. Like "Endless Buffet of Love…" or something. It did roll off the tongue better than the option Stanley's Italian had chosen in Peawanuck, "All you care to eat." which would make a terrible romance novel title.

Unlike his friends, Miguel had never left the area, choosing to get his online degree in spatial physics and math from online schools and work remotely. Lately, however, he had noticed that his friends had not moved away so much as they had, really, disappeared.

And he hadn't, really, heard anything from them.

He sat there in that Diner often thinking about them. Especially on the weekends. Eventually he noticed something that entirely occupied his thoughts and kept him coming back over and over.

The average serving for breakfast of scrambled eggs was about 4.5 ounces, a big serving spoonful, so about 3 eggs, give or take. The 6x12"' serving trays were about 4 inches deep, so they held about 120 ounces of Egg, or close to it, since the tops were not rounded or overflowing.

This means that each pan could hold enough to serve about 27 people before it needed to be replenished. He took note that, on a busy day, there were that many people through the buffet every hour.. But the eggs were not replenished,

That's when Miguel remembered the mug and the promotion.

A Bottomless cup of coffee. He hoped that his friends, wherever they were, still had theirs as he took the pulsing tracker device in his right hand, and reached into the cup, extending his arm until the cup fit like a band around his shoulder.

He dropped the device and heard it fall.

35 -It's a Small World After All

"Over the last hundred years or so, The Disney Corporation had pissed off the aliens, kickstarted the Ape Uprising™, and been invited to serve as an envoy to the great pan-galactic court system, so it would have been easy to forget that it was, once, just a little animation company.

Tiny little animation company.

But it was.

It was founded on October 16, 1923, by brothers Walt Disney and Roy Disney as Disney Brothers Cartoon Studio. They produced cartoons with the little characters, like Mickey Mouse, Donald Duck, Minnie Mouse, Goofy, and the list goes on.

Eventually, these characters became a smaller and smaller part of their retinue of films, cartoons, live action park attractions, etc. Disney's catalog became huge, containing a wealth of intellectual property that staggered the imagination. "

"I think I already know this part," said Kyle, huddled under his ragged blanket in the cold light of the tiny fire.

"Hey, Princess Bride. Shut the fuck up. I'm telling a story, and stories have power," I shot back. Kyle could be annoying. I tried to be kind because his parents got eaten. But, realistically, not my problem,

"I don't even know what that means," Kyle huffed.

"And you never will if you don't stop talking more than you listen."

I made the mic drop motion, again to a deaf room,. Kyle had never seen a microphone or, indeed, experienced anything powered by electricity.

Stupid little Kyle.

"Can I continue?"

Kyle nodded and I picked up.

"According to some widely disseminated, but controversial legal rulings, corporations were people back then. But, in reality, they always had been. And this gave corporations great power. Some say that the corporation was the thing that beat back the old times, that permitted the clear light of the modern world to shine through. "

I was secretly a little disgusted that I had written this shit. Humanity needed a better historian. I'm just a guy with a so-so memory who wasted most of his brain power on the names of the actors from Grey's Anatomy, certainly not relevant anymore since most of them had been eaten long ago. Even Ellen Pompeo and that McDreamy.

"Disney fought hard to keep the copyrights for their characters in place, long after they even stopped using them in films and media. Many people thought it was blind commercialism that kept them beating that drum, every day, in court after court, fighting tirelessly against the day when these copyrights fell.

But years of legal battles, briefs, injunctions, etc. had to end at some point, Disney would be forced to give up eventually, and accept the progress of intellectual property law.

And today was that day, the day when the arcane restrictions of copyright expired across the planet and the giant old Gods were freed to march across the cities of the world roughly, crushing and cowing the humans in their wake while the press commented wanly, amidst all the screaming how you could see right up giant Minnie's dress. "

36 - Synthetic Research

....

Selig slid up the bar and gave the bartender a knowing look. He was completely in-period. It would have been hard, really, for anyone to see the flaws in this reproduction.

"Could I get one more of those crystal meads," Selig asked, managing his voice to match the reduction in volume across the cantina. It seemed like most of the creatures assembling tonight had left already.

"Of course, boss," the bartender filled the elaborate glass and set it in front of Selig. It wasn't large but crystal mead packed a punch.

Selig looked the bartender up and down. He was a handsome man, in his thirties, seemingly, with blue-tinged skin and a crest of tiny knobs stretching across his forehead. Selig tried to place his race and failed. But he continued.

"Can I ask you a question?"

The bartender put down his rag and nodded. In a way, everything in this holographic AR suite knew that this question was what the simulation itself was about. It's called synthetic research, to use holographic representations to generate real data.

"Sure, boss. Fire away..."

Selig looked at his hands. They were old now, with strategic wrinkles. Next to the Bartender, he seemed ruddy, though, almost salmon colored. Humans were definitely in the pink/orange/red/brown spectrum when seen alongside the other races. It was the copper in their blood.

"Do you think there can actually be real peace between the different races of the universe?"

The bartender paused. He put his hand out. "Aiko. My name. If we're going to get deep here you should know it."

Selig took his hand and shook it. Both men felt the strength of the embrace created by the magnetic surface generation that holography employed.

"Selig, nice to meet you."

Aiko smiled a bit then picked up a glass to wipe clean. "You seem like a nice guy, so I'll try and break it down. No, not in the long run. If it's a sprint, sure, you and I can drink, talk, laugh. But in a marathon, you have to be for your own people, right?"

Selig looked into his blue-black eyes. "Is that true, though? Is that always how it is?"

"Try this. If I told you that only one human at a time could be in the bar, and another human came, what would you do?"

Selig thought for a minute. "I'd try to convince you to let him in."

Aiko locked eyes with him, "You'd fight for him to be able to come in. You'd support him. I'd be the bad guy"

"That's not really…"

"It's true."

"Let me think about that. One more?" Selig moved his glass over. The cantina had fallen quiet.

"Sure. Last call."

Selig was still animated, thinking about Aiko's words. "I'll get back to you on that. You here tomorrow?"

Aiko smiled. "Every day."

With that, Selig faded away. The room melted like so much snow, leaving cold metal walls. Aiko thought about these humans.

They would fight.

37 - Dora's Friends

Kesha breathed a silly over-the-top sigh while the doll lying in the bed next to her got it all out of her system.

She remembered, as recently as last year, how surprised she was to be hearing Baby Dora's high-pitched voice coming from the doll as she talked about the day's events. The conversation soon became more lively, with Kesha joining in eventually. Soon, they had gotten incredibly close.

Kesha never thought she would have a close friend, really. Especially one that really loved her like this. And wasn't afraid to tell her.

Baby Dora continued, "I have twenty reasons why I love being with you and I can put them in alphabetical order or order of importance or really any order that works for you"

Kesha giggled a little out loud. That was a lot of reasons. She hated the idea of forcing the tiny doll to have to alphabetize things or do math or any of the things that Kesha herself disliked. The more she got to know her, the more she realized that they really weren't so different.

"How about any order that makes you feel happy?"

Kesha took Baby Dora's much smaller hand in hers and waited, just like she did way back when Baby Dora told me about how she had been found by the family at a garage sale over ten years ago way in the back, under a bunch of kitchen supplies and how she had to have her neck restricted so it was secure and provided a sturdy resting place for her pretty little porcelain head, as round and nearly as large as a newborn baby. Baby Dora told good stories.

"Ok, I love being with you because you are so much bigger and I know you would protect me." Baby Dora said, smiling widely. Kesha looked around the room and saw a safe space, one without any obstacles that might hurt the little doll, bright and open and padded everywhere that it could be padded. This was a perfect little girls' room, made for a perfect childhood.

In the back of her head, Kesha knew, however, that most dolls never talked. Most toys were quiet. It was childhood trauma, painful events, hurt, that caused dolls and toys to become friends, to speak up.

Kesha realized that she had no life, no love, no joy, before Baby Dora came into her world and she felt so grateful.

Suddenly the space between them was filled with the sounds of Suzanna at the door, her Dad swatting at her and sending her off to get ready for bed. She made a quick detour at the kitchen for a cookie then ran to her room to huddle under her covers, staring at the door, hoping it would stay closed and her father would put down the glass and wander to his room.

By the time Suzanna had fallen into a fitful sleep for the night, both the dolls had stopped talking, quiet for now, frozen.

38 - Pigeons of Jericho

· ·

To figure out how it got this far, it's important to remember that artificial intelligence tends to work due to its similarities to how organic intelligences work. It learns, grows, changes...

And it alters course sometimes.

Jericho was a next generation dynamic AI knowledge assembly tool. Or DAIKAT for short. DAIKATS were used to plan business dynamics, create paths to completion for classroom studies and, importantly, to model the interactions of nations for optimum peace and prosperity.

The term sounds very dry but it just meant that it used what it had at its disposal to to learn and grow and make decisions. And much like humans, that meant guessing sometimes. And sometimes it meant acting on a kind of, well...

...Superstition.

That isn't as nefarious as you think.

Have you ever heard of superstitious pigeons?

Well, pigeons don't have huge brains. We know this because we make fun of them all the time for it. But they are exceptionally good at pattern recognition. They recognize patterns and try to learn from them.

Unfortunately, most of the patterns occurring in the universe are what's called "trivial," meaning they don't have a clear point of causal or identifying relationship. We see that in the birth of many religious regulations. Someone cleans himself with his left hand and then wins a war. So, from now on, God wants everyone to do left handed cleaning.

These trivial patterns happen to pigeons. A pigeon might dip and shake and then be given food. So it now dips and shakes for food. The two aren't connected, but the pigeon's brain is sure they are.

So we see superstitious pigeons twitching, bobbing, dancing, moving in awkward ways, just to solicit food.

Superstitiously.

An evolving part of the human brain is committed to the task of discerning trivial from non trivial patterns. And that's important. If we have tools that can help us not fall into believing every pattern we identify, we are actually able to imagine more, to dream more, to consider things, without placing unreasonable faith in their reality.

So Jericho was built, in many ways, like a skeptical human being. Which is the problem.

Skeptics keep on trying to find proof of truth in the midst of patterns. And our brains do a decent job of it, really. We break down what works and doesn't. We decide what patterns are real and which ones are illusory.

And we program the DAIKATS to do the same thing. They're just a little better at it than us.

It wouldn't be an issue, really, if DAIKATS were only used by the US, or by the US and allies. At this point in history, they are used by everyone. So when we see a series of papers spit out by the system, we can assume, really, that other countries will get there, eventually.

Even this list here, a comprehensive one of one thousand and twenty seven magic words, one thousand and twenty five of which don't work.

39 - Advanced Chaotix

Valeri had taken on the job of being a chaotician after her programming career had crashed and burned. Apparently, Amazon hates it when you push code that randomly insults Kindle users for their taste in literature. Sadly, this was the software needed for this time in history, right, Dan Brown?

Valeri admitted that she hated Dan Brown. Sadly, for her, she considered, she was now stuck in a sort of Dan-Brown-esque dilemma.

First of all, being a Chaotician pays almost one hundred and seventy thousand dollars a year, which, after taxes, comes out to almost ten thousand a month. This was almost as much as she made at Amazon. And she suspected that the secret order of Occult Chaoticians would have a better sense of humor.

You would think?

The job was simple. Sow chaos. Apparently, there is energy in chaos. Energy that can be funneled and used. And she could feel it. When Valeri introduced that software worm into the Federal housing commission's database that gave away homes to people owned by commission members. That was a good time.

Or when she created a programmatic hook into the national database system that switched people's social security numbers with random people all over the country. This little piece of chaos actually caused a national outcry against the permanence of credit reporting. Valeri had never seen this many people rising up to abolish credit reporting in her life.

So, a move forward, she thought.

The more she invested in this work, however, the more she noticed some things about herself. She felt bigger, grander, I guess, more important in the world. I mean, have you ever created something that changed, literally, EVERYTHING?

Valeri walked, admittedly, a little taller. And this is where her mental energy went. It was often hard to focus on other parts of her life.

She was incredibly invested in being a chaotician. And to the principles of Chaotix- creating chaos that changes the world.

There was a puzzle here, something for her to solve. What were the things that people relied on, what were the ways that chaos could shake those things up.

She had few interactions with other chaoticians. But when she was able, she used the others to spread something, to pass on her viruses and ideas to sow real chaos.

It was becoming something.

And it made her wonder what the other chaoticians were working on. Science, Magic, what were their tools to work with?

The final part of the puzzle was becoming clear, though. And Valeri was impressed with its simplicity.

Every day, she found it a little harder to think as her brain got another few inches away from her spinal connection, distancing itself from her extremities and her body expanded. She was already too big to fit into most of her clothing.

By this time next month, she imagined, her lumbering, mindless body would be many times larger than this building, and the ensuing chaos would be visible, probably, from space.

40 - The Marigana

About twenty years ago, the fantasy author Kendra Mieda started painting

The details of this painting came from her books, young adult novels that had captured the imagination of the whole world with their fantastic stories of hidden worlds, magic, insane creatures, and of objects of such important that they were worth killing for.

These objects were all part of something she called the Yuritage Codex, and they included thirty seven items of incredible rarity. Each was depicted in the painting. They are:

Blah Blah Blah, am I right?

Stella erased the last paragraph. This was brutal. She had written ten books already about this beautiful and busty nymphomaniac fantasy author Kendra whose books altered reality and she was running out of ideas. More to the point she had already run out of ideas.

For the record, the Busty and Nympho parts sold books. If people had to read with one hand, that's life. No apologies. Lately, though, it seemed like Kendra was a kind of a Mary Sue. Nothing bad really had ever happened to her.

Maybe it was time for Kendra to dive in the shit.

Stella herself needed to get out of the house. Perhaps there was an idea out on the hot cement of the big city.

Mentally, Stella erased that. Holy God, she sucked today.

There is a concept in Japan called "Magic Room" where you accidentally walk into a store or room or something that you never saw before. And then you buy something or find something magical, and the room or store disappears.

Maybe that could happen.

That would be fun. She could write about that. Or maybe she would just step in dog shit. Kendra could do that. And then, afterward, while wiping it off her shoe she discovers that there is a magic genie in her shoe and she's rubbed it.

And out comes the foot genie.

She saw a sushi place and stopped in. Stella was a vegetarian, but she loved a little Miso soup and a couple Tamago. Lots of Ginger.

As the older man came with the check, she tried something.

"Excuse me, sir, do you have a back room with magical objects all over?"

The waiter looked at her just for a second. "Of course. It's right back there."

Stella had seriously not expected that.

"Wait, you do?"

"All sushi places do. Americans never notice. Americans Stupid."

Suddenly, Stella was grateful she hadn't written this guy.

Embarrassing.

She stepped in the back room. There wasn't much here. In fact, most of the room was taken up by two doors.

"This is door to go home. This door goes through the Marigana. It takes you to knowledge."

Stella needed knowledge, for sure, otherwise she'd lose this book deal. But, admittedly, this looked way sketchy.

She walked through the Marigana and saw Kendra's home in front of her. It was exactly like she had written. Stella took a deep breath.

Maybe something really bad had to happen to Kendra.

41 - Giving In

Since she was a little girl, Stacy liked to be the aggressor when they played.

Evan lived next door and it was soon clear that his crush was only amplified by her dominance. As children, it manifested in ways that were endemic to children. It was always her in the lead, where they went, where they ate, whose house they would go to after school, even what days they might play hooky from school, running half clothed in the waves at the beach, hiding underwater from any passing adults, in love with summer.

He followed her to high school, to sit behind her whenever possible. Stacy loved putting her hand on her neck, behind her, and feeling him reach out and touch it. She knew he thought about her.

She knew he dreamed about her.

Stacy's long, kinky black hair wove a ring around her when she danced, exploded from her head like the foliage from a tree, and, every year, during the summer, when she began to get hot, coiled around her in braids, wound the way she liked, a way that Evan learned to do for her in the 12th grade.

Evan wrote her poems, innocent at first, but more elaborate and sensual as they got older. He never denied Stacy anything. Any physicality, any invasion, any transgression was welcome. Stacy learned to kiss using his lips, his face, at her leisure. And when she felt like pursuing any curiosity, Evan's body would always be available to her.

One night, when he was nineteen, Stacy, awake and warm in her home next door, climbed into his window. She had had a key to Evan's home since the third grade, but that didn't matter. She found him in bed and pulled the covers down. He woke up to her hands loosening his pajamas. She was quiet and it was so dark. In the dim light of her phone's flashlight, she wanted to see what a boy looked like naked, aroused.

Evan stood and let her remove his pajamas, sliding them down as he made himself aroused for her.

That summer, she climbed into his bed nearly every night. And he did what she wanted.

On the last night before college, she came with a tool to penetrate him, to own him. She pulled off his underwear and laid him down on the bed on his belly.

And she used him for hours.

Afterward she turned him over to kiss his neck.

She felt Evan squirm a bit beneath her as her incisors digged into the soft flesh below his chin. He didn't panic. He gave into her willingly, well past the point where he had to know it was real.

His hands wrapped tightly around her waist and he inhaled the vanilla scent of her nape while the life poured out of him for her Sagrado coming of age ritual, where the very first victim, the first food the vampire would ever taste, had to be a willing sacrifice.

42 - The Viper in the Shell

The Kaigara was the largest project ever engaged in, requiring the vigorous participation of every one of earth's allies and it was very nearly done.

It was a Dyson sphere built around a neighboring star, completely enclosing it, with the sphere's inner surface to be in the constant light of that sun, and all the energy from it absorbed. The massive outer surface would be thick enough to produce its own gravity - with some help - letting animals and flora live on the inside.

The surface area would be five hundred and fifty million times the surface area of the earth. And it could be used to grow food and resources for every alien race participating. An undertaking like this might take hundreds of thousands of years to accomplish, but thanks to the participation of Tau Raza, a race capable of time travel, the process began two hundred thousand years ago.

And it would be finished next week.

In one of the earth languages, Kaigara meant shell. And it would be a shell, but it would be so much more.

The Talokians, another friendly race, offered technology that enabled them to replicate plants and organics needed to seed the shell once it was built. The Venn, an alien species man had also befriended, came up with ways to transfer spirits there, into newly made bodies, when it was ready. Teleportation technology would create portals to help the various planets gain access to the wealth provided by the shell.

And a technology invented on earth, Feynman Distillate, a form of matter that cuts off the passage of time, could be used to store what's needed until it was used to build.

A project like this depended on the fact that Earth had many allies and made friends among the stars. In fact, mankind had only ever encountered one warlike alien race, the Villi, passionate about expansion, determined to destroy them. And they nearly had, carving the symbol for their species, two bars with a crossbar, across the very earth and destroying three major cities.

Humanity had managed to repel them at a price.

But today, just a week away from the completion of the shell, that price, the cost of being in a global community, seemed so very minimal. It seemed like such a powerful message to the people and races involved. These are the dividends of peace.

The shell would pay off for centuries, with a wealth of resources that could never be tapped completely.

As emissaries from all the alien species stood watching, the final parts of the framework surrounding the shell were removed by robots. The shell itself shifted into focus and millions of cameras switched on to record these first few moments.

As it turned, the main viewer showed two bars with a crossbar etched into the inside of the shell, the result of the latticework needed to build the planet, showcased on an open plain in the center of what they realized was the original Villi homeworld.

43 -The Life in the Light

I read somewhere that human beings are capable of touching the infinite in two areas- in their ability to love and their equally infinite capacity for suffering.

I agree with that.

And when I tell you that they often happen together, it's out of experience. I've watched it. Hell, I've been it. But I have hope and it's all based on something I saw through the doorway when I was seven years old.

Oh, you can tell me all day long that it wasn't real, but I know it was.

My mother was dying of breast cancer. That still happens today, despite the millions of pink ribbons in circulation. Crazy, I know. But somehow, cancer sneaks around those ribbons and it bites you.

Or stabs you. This is metaphorical, so i don't really have any idea how cancer does what it does in this sort of narrative personification. If cancer were a person, he would be a dick.

So, I guess he dicks you.

Whatever.

Jeanie would think that was hilarious. But she hasn't really said anything in a few weeks. She doesn't have much time left. It's a different kind of cancer than mom had, but it's just as deadly.

I'm here because there is no place else to be. Jeanie was sixteen years old, standing next to me at the door. She saw it, too. How my father took my mother's hand and held it. He moved their fingers in a certain way because she could no longer move. And then it happened.

This blue light swept over them, it seemed to illuminate them from the inside out. I could see it. To us it looked like something nearly magical, alien. And we both agreed years later we saw the same thing. In the light, they were both transformed. They got younger and younger. Until they were both barely teenagers. Then, the light flared to white. And they disappeared.

Leaving this wave of peace behind.

If Jeanie hadn't been there, I would never have believed it. From then on, she took care of me. She was a mom and a dad and a best friend and my favorite teddy bear all in one.

She was my world.

We never were able to figure out the light, what it was or what THEY were, Mom and dad. But they were part of us. And we are part of them.

And I believed.

I've been here every day, working, watching, waiting for the moment. And it helps me remember every great moment where Jeanie was the biggest thing in my heart.

And no matter what happens next, I'm ready.

So, I slide into the chair next to her and I reach out my hand to touch hers the way i saw through that door almost sixty years ago. I position our fingers the way I remember as I look into the eyes of my only sister and wait for the light to take us.

And it's beautiful like I remember.

44 - Autopay

"Is that a phone? Don't touch that."

"It's a phone store, dude. Everything in here is a phone."

Zack slumped over a little. "I mean not a working phone. Like, don't call anyone." He waved the gun around..

Willow held her gun pointing at the floor as she cradled her nine months pregnant belly. "None of you call anyone."

"Can I text my mom and let her know I'm ok?" asked the nonchalant goth girl in the corner.

Zack really thought that the no calling rule would imply a no texting rule. How neurodivergent were T-mobile employees?

"Can you not? We're trying to do something here."

"Are you robbing us?" The pale girl by the front desk asked. Her name tag had a question mark on it. What the hell kind of customer service was that? It really pissed Zack off.

"So, question girl, honey, what is your actual name?" Willow beat him to the punch.

The girl looked confused and then laughed. "Oh, yah. I hate it when the customers get all 'hey, I know your name' and shit."

"Then why wear a name...? You know what? Nevermind." Zack moved to the middle of the room, and addressed the three employees.

"Listen up, people. Who here knows how to use that computer?"

The three of them actually just looked at each other, confirming, for Zack and Willow, the very special hiring policies of phone service stores everywhere.

"Anyone?"

"I mean, I can log in and sell you a phone," responded the tall kid with the perpetually confused look.

Willow stepped up. She was about half his height, but round and angry. 'Can you wipe our bill?"

"I don't think so," intoned tall guy as he peered down at her.

"I will fucking eat your kneecaps if you look at me like that again, Godzilla."

Zack tried to be the voice of reason, "Look, this is simple. You guys billed us twice. Autopay. So the rent bounced. Now we live in a Kia. Living in a Kia is pain. So you have to fix it.

"I do not know how to do that," replied Godzilla

"That is impossible," spoke up goth girl.

Willow was livid. She lifted the gun up, " Really? Because I live in a Kia, bitch. The car of infinite possibility."

"Can we call the manager?" asked the nameless one.

"Please. Ignore my very first order and just call anyone you like right now. Want to make a reservation at Nobu? Call the joke line?" Zack tried unsuccessfully to keep his voice from doing that squeaky thing.

"Only managers can change bills."

"I just do not think that is true." Zack countered, looking at Willow. Maybe it was true. She shrugged back at him. They should have come up with some cool hand signals. If they ever buy a couple guns from his brother and hold up a store again, they definitely will.

Question Girl noted, "hey, the floor is wet,"

Zack and Willow looked down.

"Oh shit"

45 - Fathers and Sons

Jesus' third and youngest son, Emmanuel, often came dangerously close to suggesting that he was god, something Jesus himself had warned him against.

Emmanuel was a kind boy, easy-going and loving, but he could be intense at times. He spent most of his time feeding and clothing people, helping them meet their basic needs, elevating them, and for that, Jesus was very proud. Out of all his children, Emmanuel had sort of followed in the "family business."

Oh, Jesus and Mary Magdalene were proud of all their children.

Noura, their eldest, was a powerful advocate for young mothers and had changed the way that the people of Paddam Aram responded to childbirth. As a midwife and healer, she had proven to be essential to the health of the entire area. And Bihram was a stonecutter and workman who had helped build some of the most beautiful structures all over the city. His artistry lifted people's spirits and souls.

Jesus often thought that he was prepared for how much he loved his children but had never become ready, really, for how much he liked them. The times when he could just enjoy his family's company, to wallow in the silliness that invariably came to the surface when they were all together, the bad jokes, the simple meals filled with easy conversation and the late night glasses of wine, chased by laughter, these were the best times of his life.

And Mary herself had grown even more impossibly lovely and quirky with the passage of time. She had never lost the passionate playfulness that drew her to be a sex worker in her youth or her easy love of people. But the quick, clever, yet always non-judgmental humor that had shown its face from time to time in her youth was now a seasoned and willful banter that propped up every moment he was lucky enough to spend with her. He considered himself lucky each time he had opportunity to wash and massage her feet, which still, after years together, led to an evening to remember.

But despite their good fortune, Jesus' past haunted him in bits. Like today when the Pharisees proclaimed publicly to admonish Emmanuel, calling him his "father's son" in a text that demanded he stop likening himself to God. Emmanuel would not stop, Jesus knew. His entire message was that they were all god, each person a temple of their own, worthy of worship and respect.

Jesus had listened on a number of occasions to Emmanuel's take on his own personal theology in joy. He loved how the young man had passionately placed his faith in people, in love, in the power of service. He wished he had been as eloquent as he.

And today, he tried his best to channel that eloquence. He pulled on his best robes. He would go down to the temple and meet with the Pharisees with Emmanuel.

He would defend his son the way he wished his father had done for him.

46 - True

....

Mairi MacGillivray was nearly seventy-years old, but she looked about thirty-five. With her magics, it was no great difficulty to look on the outside as she felt on the inside, in her mind's eye. It is how she easily walked, wand in hand, through the markets in Edinburg, when her infant self had been paralyzed. This was her true self now.

After all, in magic, being true to yourself is always important.

Mairi was far from the tiny thatched home where she was born and even farther from the beautiful castle where she now lived. The truth was that she was out looking for someone she had only seen in paintings.

Along the way, though, Mairi filled her bag with barley, kelp, kale, and even some sweets for later. Even the greatest musicians in the world didn't pass on the chance to shop at a fresh market.

She admitted to herself that everything smelled amazing.

But as she reached for the potatoes, she saw her, across the market. She was laughing with a friend, but there was no doubt in Mairi's mind it was her. The same shock of red hair rested on her head. She was slim, but muscular and quite pretty. Mairi stood up taller to walk her way.

This was a great hero of Scotland.

And Mairi had a proposition for her.

Scotland was filled with men and women who had valiantly fought the English, people who were willing to give all for Scotland as William Wllace had in her youth. Mairi fought, as well, in her own way, training the Children of Scotland who were attuned to magic in its occult ways.

Her own training had begun with manifesting her body as she saw it. And it was how she began training for the children. Her children were proud scots and they knew of heroes like Cumhachdach and Lachlan "Ghualainn Leathann", the broad shouldered. These were men who fought and died, who gave everything they could for their home.

Despite the fact that they were not born men.

Mairi knew that these powerful men, fighters, statesmen, were born women. If anything this added to their valor. They could have easily stepped aside and let the men fight. No one would have denied them that. But instead, they put on the clothing of men and picked up the swords of men and fought and died that way.

Mairi and the children she taught knew of their secret valor behind the valor. And it was the children who suggested she ride out today.

She stood next to the woman that the English had called a red-haired witch in insult. It was clear to Mairi that she was no witch. But just as clear that she was a woman of immense power.

Mairi made the offer to her, to use her magics to change her body from the man she was born to the woman she saw inside.

And the great hero of Scotland paused and considered her truth.

47 - The Unicorn

....

"Do you guys want to get some calamari?"

Linda replied, "I don't eat anything with a face."

Lucy stared. She wasn't 100% sure squids had faces.

"Kidding. that sounds good." Linda looked at the rest of the menu.

Lucy and Neal hadn't been on a date since Eddie moved out to go to San Francisco to be with his new Prog-Rock band. They all promised to stay in touch, but it was hard to tell what might happen. They had never been left for four grown men and a drum machine before. They had met Linda online and this would be their first in-person meeting. Neal read his menu. "I think there is a section here for just faces. Deep fried faces."

Linda laughed, "You guys have a better menu than I do."

Lucy picked up the wine menu, "Guys, grapes died for these. Let's fuck up a bottle."

A glass of wine all around later, they had managed to order. Lucy spoke up," That was kind of exhausting, guys. I need a nap."

Neal, 'Yeah, when was the last time we restauranted?"

Linda jumped in, "ok, mom and dad, you don't get menus anymore.

Lucy countered, "That was rude." and flicked a little water at her playfully

Linda looked play aggressive. "When you least expect it, Lucille."

Lucy had always liked the way that people called her that when they were serious, or challenging. It was like her super hero name.

Neal started, "So, technically, we are here looking for a unicorn, is that something you are ok with?" In the poly world, a third, especially a pretty girl, was considered a unicorn. Hard to find. Legendary.

Linda took a drink. "Ok. Cat, say goodbye to bag. Here goes. I am, actually, a unicorn."

Lucy asked, "So, wait, you are already in a relationship?"

"No. I'm actually an enchanted mythical creature. During the day I can appear human, but at night, I am a horned enchanted horse who can fly."

Neal paused, "Get the fuck outa here." They all laughed.

Linda continued, "I'm serious. That's why I answered your ad. I'm sick of hiding."

Wait, so you are an enchanted unicorn AND you just happen to be looking for a couple to date?"

"I know, crazy, but where do you think the term comes from?"

"I'm positive that's not it," said Lucy

Linda grabbed a roll, "Well, it could be."

Neal chimed in, "ok, so you are a mythical creature. What do you eat?"

"When I'm human, really, anything I like. In my Unicorn form, mostly apples."

Lucy looked intent. "Mostly apples, huh?"

"You don't believe me. That's fair. We can wait until tonight."

"So, are all unicorns female?" This seemed like the right question for the moment, Neal thought.

"Oh No," Linda added. During the day, as a person, I'm all woman. But as an enchanted horse creature I'm definitely male."

Lucy spit out her water. It was only three blocks from home and almost dark.

"Check, please."

48 -Returning

....

If they had to do it all over again, Tom wouldn't have lost his temper and choked their daughter, Emily, to death that night, when she was eleven.

And Audra, if she had had time to think about it at the time, she probably wouldn't have helped him hide the body and cover it up for him.

But they did. And that was something they had to live with.

Until she showed up at the door fifteen years later, almost to the day, ushered in by the sheriff, a man who had never given up looking for her, convinced she was kidnapped.

They put on a good show. They hugged her, they cried, and they gave thanks to god for bringing her home. They had kept her room exactly as it was, more out of inertia than anything else.

You see, they had been acting for years. The two of them had been performing, pretending, faking the longing for their kidnapped daughter to finally return home. They were not wealthy, but they had offered rewards, made public appearances, tried to look, to all viewers, like hopeful parents exercising every ounce of strength they had not to lose themselves in their grief.

Emily didn't seem to remember anything of her time away. Or her death. She hugged them back, kissed them, languished in their putative long lost love and affection.

That night, after the sheriff left, the three of them sat at home.

Audra brought dinner to the table, staring at her newly returned daughter. Her hands shook as she put the platter of chicken down on the table, and she almost dropped the lemonade. Tom got up and stepped away to the bathroom, for longer and longer periods of time, until, finally, he left dinner altogether. Emily appeared to not notice.

Just being with family again was enough for her.

She seemed to have no expectations, no hopes, no idea of what she wanted. She was quiet, inscrutable. And as the evening wore on she became even quieter.

Tom stared at her from the kitchen as she sat, unmoving in the living room chair facing the television. Audra stepped up behind him and held his hand.

It was trembling, too

Emily turned toward them, her eyes lit red like crimson bulbs in their sockets. She stood up and moved toward them, her feet unmoving, propelled by something infernal, something invisible.

The blood ran from their faces as Emily's mouth opened and her jaw unhinged. She leaned forward in a quick spastic motion and ripped their heads off.

That was the day they had to experience every day, over and over again. Not the fateful day they killed Emily, because that was a mistake.

It was the day that never happened. A day when they were discovered, when they could have admitted it and begged for forgiveness, where they would have had the chance at redemption, a chance they lost when they both died, peacefully in their sleep, in their eighties.

49 - The Host

Aria sat on the edge of the roof the way it used to drive her parents crazy when she was alive.

She was nude but the arc of her wings as they wrapped around her cut her off from any prying eyes that may have been looking. She felt the wind play off the tiny hairs that stretched across her belly, light like down feathers.

And despite the light chill in the air it warmed her from inside.

She often flew naked over humans letting their eyes linger on her very obvious assets, knowing that the terrors of the end times themselves couldn't stop human beings from wanting her, from exploring in their minds.

She knew because she WAS human. Aria was one of those girls who matured early, whose chest and the sharp jutting curves of her hips exploding below her lithe waist made the adults around her nervous. They called her slut and whore and berated and body shamed her for what they fantasized he was up to in those minds. She was branded a whore before she had ever had the requisite sexual contact with anyone. So she did what a lot of girls in her situation did.

She threw herself into it.

She reveled in sex, enjoyed it. She would never control how people treated her, the names they would call her. So she didn't bother. And when the first fallen hacked the system and killed god and all the angels, she found herself reborn as part of the new angelic host - an Angelum.

Aria Spencer. The one everyone called ho. Aria Spencer, the girl all the guys in eighth grade had paid twenty dollars each to see her tits out behind the Sonic next to the Gym.

It made her laugh every time she thought about it. And every time she took to the air over the last fifty years, since she was remade, she laughed, too. Her new life was light and it let her lift herself above the petty judgments of human beings.

She lifted the flute to her lips and made the call. Kai and Kemir appeared above her head, red leathery wings engaged like sails letting them float down to the roof easily. She laughed at her mortal enemies as they began to disrobe, pulling off their demonic armor.

They were beautiful, with reddish skin and dark soulful eyes. She placed her hands in the center of Kai's chest.

What Aria was starting to realize was that the rules she grew up with were changing.

Under Yahweh there would have been epic wars that lasted for centuries. They would have fought and killed the Kairos and Lucifer himself. Along the way, many of the Angelum would have died, too.

She kissed Kai while she felt Kemir's rough hot breath between her legs. She could feel it inside. Yahweh was gone and in his place, one of the newer gods, making new rules, finding new ways.

And she would not be denied.

50 - Compromises

....

We live in a society of compromises, thought Zack as he tried to get his hand as far up the slot of the hospital vending machine as it would go before his wrist snapped like a birch tree sapling.

Two dollars and fifty cents for a cliff bar in a hospital was a human rights offense. Maybe that was Zack's eternal punishment, to come up, shoulder to shoulder, against the greatest minor injustices modern society had to offer and let them all reach up his butt, muppet-like, and work his wide-ass mouth.

Willow had been unconscious for about an hour, sleeping it off, and he missed her already. She was a sassy little bitch but she was his sassy little bitch and she tolerated him in the sexiest, most beautiful way he had ever imagined a woman would obliquely tolerate his bullshit ever. He was progressively more and more pleased that he had managed to slam a baby up her as he assembled his armful of premium vending machine goodies for her enjoyment upon awakening.

He may have dropped a snickers bar on the way back to the room, but the police officer handcuffed to his other arm picked it up.

"Hey, cop." Zack asked, "Why didn't you stop me from robbing the vending machine?"

"Well, one, it's Mike. You know that. And B, do I fucking look like the vending police?"

"I hear many people die from being crushed by those fucking things every year."

"Yeeeeah, well, that would be on you, great hunter. I'm supposed to stop you from running off, not from getting your ass flattened."

Zack and Willow had held up a cell phone store that morning, trying to get them to remove the excess billable charges that had caused their rent check to bounce and Emil, their dirtbag landlord to kick them out. Right now, they were in custody. Their newborn son, however, was technically free and could help stage a break at any moment, once he stopped shitting green goop into his tiny diaper. Liberation.

The head of the company himself had shown up at the store as the ambulance carried them away. Willow's water had broken right there and some idiot employee had slipped in it and hit his head, becoming, potentially, even more brain damaged.

That was the true cost of crime.

Willow had been busy creating life all over the back of the paramedic vehicle so it was up to Zack to negotiate for them both with the president of the company, who chose, inscrutably, to ride in back with them to the hospital.

But now, Zack looked down at the birth certificate and wearily signed it under the spot that listed his newborn son's first name, the one they compromised on to avoid jail time. The joke was on them, though, because that wasn't his actual signature. He was sure some future anal-retentive notary would recognize it.

For the moment, it was time to take little T-Mobile Michael Masterson home.

51 - Your Future is in The Tank

LifeQuest was originally begun, as a company, to appeal to consumers who just wanted to live forever. They grew bodies devoid of consciousness in a lab, each tailored perfectly to the needs of a client, each one a "blank," ready to be imprinted with the mind of anyone who could afford it.

Eventually, the market asserted itself.

Sure, some people wanted to live forever.

But that wasn't the bulk of the customers who walked through those big gray doors., People wanted, not just more like, but more from life.

And sure, LifeQuest had a year or two when Blanks, made sentient by the residue of past users, came alive on their own and killed people, but what company hasn't had their share of drama.

Curt called it their "Tylenol Moment," as he went through the books. And just as Johnson & Johnson survived, as a company, a few poisoned product placements on pharmacy shelves,, LiifeQuest would prevail over a few hundred pointless murders committed by homicidal vacant bodies.

The market forgets easily.

Curt was the last one out of the office pretty often. He had no wife, husband, family, or even a dog so he found himself in really no rush to skate home after a long day at work. His HR folder was full of commendations for his commitment to his job, a commitment that often found him alone at night, wandering the LifeQuest halls.

He fingered the cards in his pocket. They were perfect. And the reason that every part of this was perfect was Curt's unerring attention to detail. IIronically, this was something he was looking forward to leaving behind. Curt was tired of being this midlevel manager his whole life.

The truth is, he was a midlevel manager of life before he had anything to midlevel manage. And he'd had this haircut, the one that showed off his bald spot on top, since Junior year of high school.

Life owed Curt a little more. And life had been stingy as fuck, he thought.

He coughed as he made his way, alone, into the basement, choking a little on the cough he had had since he was fourteen, although he'd never smoked, tripping over the giant feet he'd been born with, the gangly legs, the uncoordinated gait that ever kept him from playing sports.

He stopped at the bottom, noting that all the exercise he'd tried throughout his life hadn't made him any more capable on stairs.

He looked at the card.

It said Emilé Rossai and Curt had thought long and hard about that accent mark. It made her exotic, foreign, exciting. Everything Curt wanted to be. He looked down in the tank.

In one week, he would be on the beach in Corfu, a fruity umbrella drink in that hand, seven hundred million dollars in the bank, flirting with handsome Greek men and never again managing anything, while Curtis Johnson went down in history as the first man to embezzle a million dollars and a body.

52 - The Verdent Glen Ghost Story

Scoutmaster Alvin stood up and moved toward the fire so that the light would create that eerie effect under his nose and chin that had traditionally proven to be so terrifying during ghost stories in scouting sleepaways for decades.

Alvin's uniform bulged a bit at the waist and threatened to pop while his hair, white now and thinning at top, made it clear that he was past his ghost story prime but his voice rang out in the night, still young and powerful, and his hands were as animated as they had always been.

"The boys stepped one at a time from the bus carrying their bags onto the campground where they each, in unison, set up their tents, unaware of the oncoming storm and news of a serial killer in the area, dismissed out of hand by unwitting campground authorities."

"So, wait, there was a storm coming AND a serial killer?" asked Drew, a little round scout at front.

"Yep. big storm coming, and, remember, they had heard that there was a serial killer in the area."

Marky, an older boy raised his hand and shot out, "That sounds odd, though, right? I mean, if you knew there was a serial killer, why would you just send a bunch of kids out to camp in little green tents?"

Alvin smiled. He tried to maintain his spooky ghost story voice, "No doubt, young Marky, it was a BAD DECISION." These last two words he accented as though they were the title of the ghost story. His voice wavered eerily.

The boys laughed and went "woooo", the universal response in the night for scary stories everywhere.

"As the night drew closer, the storm began to worsen. Soon, the rains had darkened every tent and sent every scout to huddle near the fire, still raging under the simple communal structure in the center of camp."

"So they were now all in the same place?" called out Erik, a skinny scout who rarely spoke. It made Alvin happy that even Erik was so engaged. He picked up the tone and advanced in an even more cartoonishly scary voice."

"Oh, yes, Young Erik. They were all assembled so closely that the serial killer, watching from the woods, could almost smell the aggregate musk of their rain soaked uniforms."

"Gross," called out the group in a silly baritone. They knew how to respond to this part. Alvin laughed.

"Oh it was gross, to be sure. But the truly gross part was to come."

They all yelled out, "Grosser," and giggled around the warmth of the fire.

The red orange sunrise started to paint the tree-line and the sound of birds faded up as though someone had turned a knob.

Alvin let himself drop to the simple stone he had used as a chair for the last thirty years, one night a year, when he came to this clearing to watch over his boys, since that fateful night when they had all died on his watch.

53 - Dollar Saver Arms Race

....

"Wait, so that is the plot of Cats?"

"We think, no one really knows for sure."

"That's dumb, somebody knows."

"No, she's right, I think. I heard that no one really knows what the plot of it, actually?"

"Is this the movie or the broadway musical?"

"I think it's both. Both of them."

"Hey, you know that you guys are getting paid for this?" Sterling poked his head into the break room and tried his best to sound motivating, not petty."

"I think this is a state mandated wellness break," countered Synthia. She had trained in an HR seminar last year. The store paid for it.

"Yeah, we're trying to get well," added Rose, taking her bra off under her shirt in that awkward torso-only dance that women did.

Sterling was eighty percent in the room now, "Why are you taking off your bra?"

Amanda shot back, "Are you allowed to talk about our underclothing?"

"She's literally taking it off while we're talking."

"I'm trying out different bra sizes like it says in that Vogue article and this one's too tight. I'm freeboobing it."

"Please do not freeboob the register."

"Too late. It's already off."

Sterling remembered back to when he had hired Rose at the Dollar Saver. That was the same day that motorcycle took his mirror off in the parking lot. What a gift that day was.

He thought he'd try this again.

"Synthia, I need you to stock today."

The women groaned and spoke up. Claire was the first one to object.

"You know you can't keep doing this."

Synthia looked unphased, "You know, I don't mind, you guys."

Rose spoke up, "No, it's just not right. In a lot of ways this is just like slavery."

Sterling rolled his eyes, "Oh my god, she's being paid. Hell, she's being paid for this argument."

Synthia looked amiable, "This isn't an argument."

Amanda shot up, "No, this is an argument. And Rose is right. Slavery was abolished."

"Do you guys actually know what slavery is? I mean, did you learn about it in school at all?" Sterling was wishing he'd skipped work today like his son had begged him to, to play nerf."

"Slavery," Claire called out.

"You can't just keep saying a word. That's not an argument."

"Solidarity!" Rose and Amanda said in unison. That was pretty cool, Sterling thought.

Synthia tried to broker peace, "Guys, thank you for standing up for me. But, really, I don't mind. If I stock today, will you stop obsessing over Rose's underwear?"

Sterling felt his heart sink. Nerf sounded really good.

"That sounds like a great deal. Thank you," It was all in stone now.

He sighed.

As the women went back to work, Sterling watched Synthia gracefully slide down the center of aisle 7 dragging the cart behind her, each arm placing product perfectly, row after row.

It was a good demonstration why Dollar Saver was succeeding in the market when other stores who hadn't hired cephalopods were not.

54 - 54

....

"So what's with the letters?"

"What Letters?"

"here," Jonah pointed at the robot's posterior.

"Jesus, Pissmonster, It's a number. She's the 54th version."

Jonah stood up straight, "Dude, can you not call me that?"

Jonah really had to pee after a party in college but, as part of the previous evening's drunken pranks, his urethra had been partially superglued. He ended up freaking out and running all over the apartment, spraying piss in such a way that it just made more sense later to move out than clean. Doreen had nicknamed him pissmonster after that. As you might imagine, it stuck.

"I'm going to call her Doreen," intoned Jonah.

"Yeah, I'm not gonna do that." Ted was actually still dating Doreen on and off. So naming his new sex robot after her was a non starter. In fact, she was on her way.

Jonah ran his fingers over her belly. "So, who is going to have sex with her first?

"Not it," Ted said as he wiped her down.

"Why did you make a sex robot if you don't plan to fuck it, Theodore?"

"I didn't make it for me. This is going to change everything. It's going to make the world safer from crazy incel men," Ted had a whole dissertation about this. He wanted to liberate women from the pawing advances of men they didn't want and still, at the same time, help manage problems with men who were becoming radicalized in a world where women were, frankly, sick of their shit, and giving up on men.

"I'll find someone." 54 was beautiful. Her features were lithe and catlike and pretty, with skin that was just a little more red than human skin, and eyes that were dark and sexy. She had short black hair in a little french pixie cut and her breasts and ass were perfect. The thing Ted was the most proud of, however, was the perfectly formed cleft between her legs, supple, with thick lips and a visible clit, the kind of shape that drove men crazy, that made someone built to, well, you know, to fuck.

"I kind of want to, kind of don't want to, but kind of don't want anyone else to. Like, I feel like she's my sister." Jonah had been over every night Ted had worked on this project.

"If so, stop feeling up her tits."

"I can't help it. This is good work." Jonah kept squeezing them casually.

Ted wiped off his hands and moved toward the door as the buzzer rang, "That's Doreen now. We're going out tonight so here's your chance, brother.."

Doreen came in, long red hair falling out of a white hat. She was fascinated by the project. She kissed Ted and winked, "Have you turned her on yet?"

"Just about to," laughed Ted

54 came to life and looked up, taking in the room. She turned to only Doreen and with a soft, sultry voice spoke up,

"Oh my god. You are beautiful."

55 - Rising Star

Amatiya was already on the party plane when Roan and Sheron got there. They quickly covered up their surprise and tried to make sure the young singer was comfortable as the private jet lifted off and headed for Ibiza.

For months now, it had been their job to manage her appearances, her outward persona as the world saw her. Today, though, she easily owned the room, followed by fans and groupies, she was bigger than life, surrounded by a newly formed entourage that seemed nearly impenetrable, committed to having as much fun as they could with this breakout star whose last round of hits had been successive number ones on the world dance charts.

Roan regrouped with Sheron in the luxurious bathroom, a few rooms over from the party, trying to figure out what to do.

This show was vital to the rest of the tour and the health of the record. And, until tonight, it had been planned down to the most trivial of details. In the body of the plane was a holographic production system that cost virtually the entire GNP for the year of most of the countries on this tour and even the programming of the system had cost a small fortune. Roan wasn't sure but he suspected this was the most high end production tour ever in the history of mankind.

And it was going off the rails right now, 23,000 feet over the Atlantic Ocean.

They ran the water to cover up the sound of their voices but they needn't have bothered. The noise from the rest of the jet was getting louder and louder as the revelry built in intensity. They had no idea where these people had come from, any of them, but, for now, their focus was on one specific person.

They had literally never experienced anything like this before. And between them, the two had logged nearly thirty years in the music industry.

Sheron began making the series of phone calls that might get to the bottom of what was happening while Roan went next door to watch out for the star he had been tasked with seeing through to superstardom for his multi-billion dollar record label executive employers.

He made his way across the room, following the unmistakable sound of Amatiya's laughter. As he got closer, he wasn't sure exactly what to expect.

He was close enough now to smell her perfume, which surprised him.

Roan stared into her face as she exploded, throwing a bottle of rum across the room. He tried to avoid catching her eye himself as he scanned it, learned it, and tried to pierce the illusion of who the most famous icon in the pop world was, seeing, really no difference in her face than the one he had generated, through AI, just a few short months ago.

That Amatiya they had worked hard to make a star worldwide, on screens across the state, the country, the planet.

So who was this one?

56 - Bring On the Storm

Wolfie barked at every oncoming storm, her hackles up and her tiny black-furred body shaking. Tom had heard for years that dogs were a lot more perceptive than humans to slight changes in the atmosphere. They could tell when storms were coming. They could see things no one else could.

He believed it.

He went to the cabinet to fish out the dehydrated lamb hearts. She loved those. He had tried one once, last year. It was a little "organny", but he could see why she might like them. They tasted like life. It's funny how organisms on this planet were able to extract life from death, every day, taking in the essence of the world around them, growing stronger, from the simple act of death and sacrifice.

She was a little too excited for the snacks. Tom would just have to get used to her trailing around underfoot for a little bit, until the storm let up. That would normally be fine, but he did have some business downstairs to attend to. So he figured maybe he'd tire her out a little.

Out in the back, though, she seemed to go a little crazy near the back of the yard. She seemed terrified by the newly dug up weeds and couldn't even really focus on the frisbee well enough to catch it and return it. Tom remembered when she was just a puppy how she loved the frisbee at the beach. They could toss it back and forth literally for hours before she would wind down and fall asleep, head on his lap, in the car on the way back home.

Without a doubt she was the most active of all the puppies there, running in circles to burn off the calories and wear herself out. He did love watching her have fun. She was the light to his dark side, he always thought. She was the thing that renewed his faith in everything when it was at its very end and he could no longer stand to be around anyone, really.

They came in, tracking little bits of grass and mud with them.

Wolfie bit at his ankles, causing Tom to lose his balance at the top near the open cellar door.

The stairs were slick and smelled of copper as he slid down them, smashing his head into the stone floor at bottom with a dull ruddy thump. He had become too comfortable in the dark of the storms over the years, frequent storms he had used to kidnap local travelers and bring them here to carve up and play with, eventually letting them bleed out onto the cold marble.

As he died, he looked up and saw the ring of spirits surrounding him, plaintive, silent, waiting for him to join them for his own unique reward.

He could hear, in the background, Wolfie barking and he realized what she had always been barking at as the spirits reached down toward him.

And then closed his eyes.

57 - Design Levels

Like most programmers, Lee had started out as a mover. Location was the highest and most accessible design level of the universe and most found that it was the easiest to work with. She had remembered the very first thing they had moved in class, actually. It was a broom, held by Aven, and Lee had made it disappear.

She pointed their hand at it and it began to lose size in some dimension that wasn't immediately obvious.

Then it was gone.

Lee knew that one day the hand motion wouldn't be necessary. She was learning now about the different design levels of the universe and how they could be manipulated.

Waving your hands wasn't really a part of it.

About a hundred years ago, a group of people had gathered around a famous Chicago building, the Hancock, and had worked together to reprogram the area, causing the entire building to disappear. It set in motion a series of events that led to programmers being discovered - recognized all over.

Until the event itself was undone by a small group of programmers. And then, they themselves were undone by another group.

Until it was redone.

One of the design layers of the universe, the major ones, was time. And this opened the door to so much.

Lee stayed in class. She learned how to master Location, the first. Then she learned how to change the shape and form of things, the send. She learned about Energy and about thought, the third and forth. Then Time, Reality, and even the basic physical laws.

Most people would never learn the eighth and final major layer. It was far too dangerous. Lee took her time with the rest, after being told it didn't matter how long it took.

They had all the time they needed.

She would be the rare student that learned about the last layer.

She felt honored to be chosen for this, but not just a little scared. The concepts she was learning were so big, spanning the very tools that had created the universe in the first place. She ate and laughed and played with her classmates until, one day, it was her time to do what she was made to do.

She traveled back.

She built a bounding area in her mind. She had to be very careful. From a distance, she could see the group that had traveled here to stop the Chicago Event and she felt it. This was the prime timeline where they did.

Then she took a deep breath and did what she was trained to do. She felt herself unravel along with this timeline while every rule, every stitch that held it together, came undone, eliminating the travelers from history. As she faded away, she thought about the power of that final layer and how easy it might be to destroy everything.

She looked down one more time at the tiny tattoo on her hand that said "2+2=5" and everything went white.

58 - Need

....

Laurie grew up in wealth and power.

But she had none of her own.

You might know her as the granddaughter of the Hypernaut, the first of the Malkin family. The Malkins were famous for their mutations. The Malkin gene is triggered by worldwide need. And Hypernaut was the first. As a young boy, it responded to crime by turning him into the world's greatest superhero. Super fast, super strong, able to fly, and nearly invincible.

Hypernaut fought crime for almost forty years, becoming loved, renowned, and very rich along the way. It started with book deals and turned into property, land acquisitions, and more. Some say he used the incredible power of his mind to understand the workings of the stock market.

Who knows?

His son acquired his abilities as a teenager. In response to the world's problem of moving resources from place to place, his body evolved the ability to transport long distances, both himself and other things. He was very strong, agile, and capable of great endurance. He soon became beloved worldwide as well. He helped food and other resources make it to people who needed it all over the world.

And also became very wealthy and powerful. As Ultiman, he ran for office and won, sitting as president for three consecutive terms.

No one dared run against him.

His daughter, Laurie's older sister, had also demonstrated great power. As did Hypernaut's other children. And sure, one or two of them had problematic careers, but the consensus in the papers was that mankind was better off for the Malkin's and their incredible genes.

And, at eighteen, Laurie was one of the oldest Malkins who had yet to manifest. Oh, a few years ago, her cousin, Apex, had manifested his abilities at the ripe old age of 18, but he had felt a call from deep space and almost immediately went to investigate it. And her other cousin, the Cyberian, had gotten her abilities at nineteen to help take down a ring of whistleblowing hackers trying to end the Ultiman presidency.

So Laurie wasn't worried. She tried hard to pay attention to the world around her. She, more than anyone in her family, tried to stay up on current events, to learn what the world around them really looked like, really needed. She took her legacy as a Malkin very seriously and had an honest desire to help people.

Not all the Malkin were successful. That's how Laurie ended up, two days after her eighteenth birthday, visiting her cousin Virago in a short term holding facility while he was on trial for insider trading. Everyone knew he could break out at any time with his superior strength and flight, so the fact that he stayed, patiently, spoke volumes on his behalf in court.

He floated, as he always did, a few inches above the ground as they spoke. Suddenly, Laurie's genetic mutation kicked in. And Virago dropped to the ground.

And so did every other Malkin on earth.

59 - The Virgin Maker

....

"A number of years ago, a scientist, through massive amounts of trial and error, managed to discover a way, with use of sound waves, of creating a sort of targeted amnesia. It could make you forget.

But not everything. Subtle changes to the tones could impact different memories. Soon, this technology was being used all over, from apps that let people "Cheat" by forgetting, for a time, who their partner was, to sound resonant pills that let people forget certain books they had read, movies they had seen."

"Ok, I get it. So where do I sign?" Timmers was eager to get this moving.

"Ok, well, you sign here and she signs here." The Dr. pointed to a line further down the document for her benefit.

Sirena looked over the document, a bit uninterested, "S'all good. I got you, baby." She signed first and handed Timmers the Pen.

"I hope you know, I love you." Timmers signed and let out a sigh.

Siirena cupped his face and kissed him, "I know you do, baby.

"But you know, all this is just hard for me." He looked at the doctor, "It's hard."

The doctor had seen it all. Since he had opened this practice he had encountered couples like this before. Men who couldn't stand the fact that their potential partners had slept with so many men before them. All they wanted was for their partner to feel like a virgin. Many men paid top dollar to have their wives forget other men, how they felt, what they did,

What they liked.

Timmers wasn't a bad guy. He was just a bit insecure. The men who came to a Virgin Maker always were.

"I mean, it's not like this is just regular, you know. She's a beautiful woman. And she did porn."

"I did a number of porn films. One or two gangbangs."

Timmers winced when she said that. He pulled away from her a little and went on, "She escorted, had some one night stands, you know, stuff like that. I mean, It's not like I totally saved myself, but I was trying to be respectful. You know?"

The Doctor turned on the device and the sound was nearly imperceptible. The lights in the room seemed to dip for a minute. Then he turned it off. "Wow. This is all so cool. You want a coffee or something, sweetie?"

"Oh my god, yes, " Sirena squeezed his shoulder tightly.

Timmers give her a quick kiss on the forehead and stepped out to the vending machine.

"Is that all, really?" Sirena asked the doctor.

"Yup. It's that simple." The doctor started to put away his equipment.

"And he'll be ok?"

"He'll be fine. We just used shaped sound to whittle down the part of his brain that cares what you did with your body before you met. It's a lot simpler than you think." The doctor put his hand on her shoulder to reassure her.

"Now, is that cash or credit card?"

60 - Try the Chicken Wings

....

"Too fucking late, Giorgio, My DNA is in that" Zack whispered behind him as he enjoyed his lap dance.

Willow looked down at him, hands on his shoulders and smooth pregnant belly grinding up against his crotch. "I don't think he heard you, daddy."

"Well, I don't want to get a pole up my ass for groping my own girlfriend," Zack tickled her a little under the belly like she liked.

She giggled and turned to press her beautiful round perfect ass against him like she did every single time in her life right before he knocked her up. "Do you think the baby's going to be a smooth black baby stripper or a keen-eyed white garage band drummer with few prospects but a good heart?"

"Ouch," Zack felt that hit a bit close to home. "I like it better when you talk slutty. Is there a suggestion box here?"

"Oh, I'll show you the suggestion box," Willow removed her thong and continued to grind. Zack tried to make words go.

"Fuck. How are you even hotter eight months pregnant?"

"Don't get ideas on making me more pregnant. I need to get this little fucking stowaway out there on the open job market."

"What a beautiful sentiment from a young mother."

"Like you aren't here for the buffet, you fucking hobo." Willow smiled at him while she tortured him with her nipples just centimeters in front of his face.

"Some of those chicken wings, and I don't mean all of them, but some have been here since we met." Zack tried hard to think of baseball. Right now, Baseball turned him on, too. What the fuck.

"Hey, don't bad mouth the wings. They keep the fat guys coming in."

"Don't kid yourself you rotund little mega ho. Nobody is in here looking at anything but you." Willow kissed him. Zack loved the way her lips felt on his, like these perfect little pillows, sliding open and waiting for him.

He heard Giorgio yell, "Cut it out."

"Hey, you fucking doberman. I'm kissing my boyfriend. Shove it up your ass."

"That's right. Don't make me go kick your butt," Zack whispered.

"Is that so, you big tough fuck? Are you going to go fight the bad guy for me?"

"Hey, I'd do anything to kiss you one more time. I'm addicted"

Willow smiled, "Took you long enough to say you loved me."

Zack knew that this had always bothered her. "I said it when it was real. When I knew it was forever."

Willow paused. "You're a slick little fuck, Zackary."

Zack felt Giorgio grab his arm and wrench him up. "C'mon, you gotta go"

Willow glared at him, "Oh no you don't, asshole. You know he's my guy."

Giorgio pushed Zack down onto the ground, making motions to drag him out. He growled, "Is that true? Are you her guy?"

Zack nodded and took the tiny box Giorgio handed him.

On his knees, he showed Willow the ring.

"I am."

61 - A Single Day to Mourn

She walked out of her tent while the man with the surf shorts collected himself. She could sense that he felt awkward about their date and she really didn't want to make it worse. She fingered the bills in the pocket of her jeans and counted it again by feel. She didn't remember much about him but his money was real.

Across the compound, she saw a small brown dog sadly flop down in front of the tiny green Camo tent toward the edge. Diane must be sick again today, she thought, out of nowhere.

As she began walking toward the tent, she could feel the man behind her, wondering if he should say goodby, and then thinking twice about it. He was the third man today and that left her with enough to eat and to maybe take care of her friends.

She fished the apple out of her bag and entered Diane's tent. She should eat.

But Diane was unresponsive. Her hands and feet felt cold.

She jumped up and ran from the tent. Someone had to have a phone to call 911, to bring an ambulance. Ryan, in the red tent pulled out his cell phone and called while she and Oliver lifted Diane. She could feel the bedsores on her lower back and she cursed herself for not intervening sooner.

She tried to remember why she hadn't done anything. She remembered talking with Diane just this morning, holding her hand, laughing along with her. They had gone to the lake early in the day and thrown rocks.

How did she get so bad in just a couple of hours?

Everything was a blur as she waited in the hallway, where the doctor's words seemed to fall to the floor in pieces.

She wondered, as she always did, looking up at the clock as it approached twelve, why it was so hard to remember. Why it was so hard to think. The idea of Diane was consuming her tonight. But even beyond that, there was something going on, something at the corner of her mind.

She closed her eyes and started pulling at the dark corners. It felt familiar, even as it radiated the unknown. As the clock hit midnight it washed over her.

There is a story that Alitha, the goddess of love, becomes human one day a year, so she can better understand the heartaches, joys, and destruction often caused by love. All of it was rushing back now. For Millennia, it had been like this. And each time, each year, she had pledged herself to be kinder to the poor mortals in love, to understand that they were like toy boats buffeted by an angry sea and sometimes it was all they could do to right themselves.

Alitha's powers returned to her and she could feel her skin light up, glowing, as it did in the presence of love. She moved closer to the bed where Dianne lay.

She could stay a little longer.

62 - Collateral Damage

There is a lot of talk amongst Subtractionists about the Retconning that was done at Verdant Glen but no one is really willing to do anything about it. I guess this is because sometimes there just are no good choices.

Only really shitty ones.

The decision to pull the trigger on that action came from very high up but in bars all over the country, people with a drink or two in them, will agree that it was probably the right call.

It happens in warfare. The enemy hides in a church, for example, or in a food depository. And you have no choice. You have to decide what kinds of collateral damage you are willing to tolerate.

What ARE you willing to tolerate?

We all know what was supposed to happen. It's a horror story that people tell their kids.

Imagine what would happen if a president, a chief of staff, a supreme court justice, and a Federal District Attorney conspired to rape and murder an ambassador's wife, kickstarting a war that ravaged half the planet for over forty years.

It's a bit much for many people to even imagine.

But what if, right? And what if that war had caused the death of over three billion people and the loss of nearly twenty five percent of the landmass of the earth to radioactive wasteland.

And what if it wasn't over yet?

If any situation in the history of man required a retconning, this was it. But the very first round of subtractionists had failed to stop the event. They arrived, back in time, the night of the party at the white house where these four friends brutalized this woman, secure in the thought that she would never disclose what happened.

So secure in their own positions and indestructibility that they acted like monsters.

And they were indestructible - invulnerable. The subtractionists from decades in the future, equipped with superior technology were still unable to gain access before it was too late. As they faded out, they made new plans.

Now in the history of Retconning, it's rare that the first incursion or two by subtractionists have been unable to make a difference and change the toxic act that caused the disaster. But in this case, it seemed that nothing they could do could stop this.

After one incursion, the jobs held by the four men switched. After another, they were slightly less high up. After another, the act was committed in secret and it took weeks longer to discover.

No matter what they did, the war happened.

Again, I say it's rare this is necessary. But there was only one thing that had worked, and could not be undone by the opposition, as versed in time travel as they were.

And that is why, in Verdant Glenn, Indiana, out in the open air one stormy August evening, subtractionists traveled back to the past and passionlessly massacred thirty-six boy scouts camping together, leaving evidence that it was a serial killer.

63 - 63

....

Dilman turned off the overhead and flicked on the lights. "So, that's the situation."

Ted wished that Doreen had just let him come to this meeting in jeans and a t-shirt. The suit was killing him. It felt like a guy made out of Rayon casually choking him while stepping on his nutsack. "Sounds pretty fucking dismal."

The people on Dilman's team laughed. "Not at all. Just trying to let you know it will be an uphill battle.

Ted looked at 63 out of the corner of his eye and she blinked. Everything about this had been uphill. Despite all that, though, he was so proud of 63. Ted asked, "So you aren't saying that no one is going to want to fuck a sex robot?"

"No, of course not," Dilman continued, "Guy's will fuck anything. They would fuck it if it looked like a sheep. What I'm saying is that they aren't going to want their friends to know."

"So, it's in secret," Doreeen was honestly confused.

Dilman deferred to Louise, his head of marketing. The presentation they had seen was mostly hers. "Well, ok, yeah. But we live in the age of social media. It's actually hard for ANYTHING to remain secret. But for the purpose of sales, we are going to need people to be more open about it."

"Right, so, no way?" Ted looked a bit confused. Why was he here?

"It's just work, that's all. At the beginning, no one wanted people to know they were on a dating app. It took time to convince people that EVERYONE used dating apps and it didn't mean you were not attractive." Louise explained.

Dilman was animated, "Yes, for sure. We just have to put in the effort to let people know that it doesn't mean you CAN'T get laid to fuck a sex robot."

Doreen got it, "Right. So it has to be normalized."

"So, right now, it's like a fat girl, right?" Dilman continued.

Ted did a double take. "What?"

Diilman leaned in. Why do people think that they can say the offensive thing if they lean in and get quieter. "Everyone knows Fat girls are the best in bed but no one wants the world to know that they are doing it?"

"I..." Doreen could actually not talk.
Ted offered up, "I thought we'd have bigger problems, honestly. Every robot we've made seems to like girls better. They don't really... Enjoy sex with me. But we can easily reset their memories afterward."

"They like girls?" Louise asked

Doreen had been considering this a lot, "Historically, men have not really behaved in an attractive way. You know? Human women and gay men can sort of ignore it. Robots are just much smarter than that."

"So, wait," Louise said, standing up, "You're saying the Robot actually doesn't WANT to have sex with men, prefers women, and becomes a virgin again after every sexual encounter?"

Doreen nodded, "Basically."

Louise looked at Dilman. "Ok, we can work with that."

64 - Lessons

....

Jeron stepped from nothingness into the bright light of the waiting room area. She was dressed in a bright green t-shirt and a pair of faded jeans.

So,, we have a bit of a language issue here. When Yahweh was god, we wouldn't have said "Yahweh was dressed in a..."

We would just call him God.

And now that Jeron had taken the job, maybe the same rules should apply. Maybe we just call her God.

So, God walked down the hallway and let herself into room 304, where Julian was watching television in a pale blue hospital gown. He looked over and smiled.

"Ooh, Mom, this is the good part."

"What are you watching?" God pulled a chair over and looked at the screen

"They are playing every Fast and Furious ever made, in some arcane order. This is ten, I think.

"How many of those did they make?" God knew, but was making small talk.

"I'm sure you know better than I do. But infinite ones. Infinity Fast and Furious."

"How are you feeling?"

Julian looked up at her and smiled. His face was deeply lined. She knew. So he asked a question. "So, this is the same hospital?"

"Yes. This is where you died almost two hundred years ago."

Julian lowered the volume, "That is nuts."

God straightened his blankets and leaned in. "What do you want to do today?"

Julian was ready for this, "I want you to tell me what you've learned.

"What I learned? As God? Sometimes it seems like it's not much. It's gone by so fast already, these last couple of hundred years."

"What lessons do you have?" Julian was too impossibly old to have such a boyish look on his face. She laughed.

"Ok. I learned that it's easy for the other guy to unmake the stuff that the last guy made. But I also learned how to make that stuff better."

"You definitely did." Julian smiled.

"I learned that people are probably more lovable because they are confused. And when they start to know too much, they become targets for bad things."

"I get that."

"I learned that having a little boy at your side to show things to while you are learning them is something every God should have. He will keep you sane and keep you honest. And keep you happy."

"I'm glad. But you are happy, even without me?"

"And I learned that every living thing has to find a way to be happy on their own, because unhappiness is a cancer. It eats you, no matter who you are."

"Even God"

She looked down at him with tears forming in her eyes."

"Even God."

"I wanted to thank you for everything. This has been crazy. I'm glad we're family."

"Are you quoting Vin Diesel?"

"I can't help it. These movies are so good."

And God let her hands fall to his all-too-familiar chest as she learned today the hardest lesson-

How to let her children die.

65 - The Legacy of the Coma Diet

If you look through Wikipedia, it will tell you the whole story, on certain select holidays before the LifeQuest marketing team rewrites it.

I mean, the page is long enough already.

At one point in history, Lifequest was an organ recovery company, helping people live longer through organ donation. Today it is a multi-billion dollar corporation helping people live better lives through use of what has been now known as "Blanks"- perfect, beautiful bodies that people could transfer their consciousness to for a time.

Oh, they've had a few problems in the past few years, but the demand for what LifeQuest has to offer is so high, people tend to gloss over the mistakes and media exposés.

The same went for its parent company, Coma Diet inc.

Humans had become complacent and flabby. And the hyper wealthy were sometimes even more complacent. And more flabby.

Coma Diet was simple proposition. Come on down and give us 2 months of your life, their ads said. They then put you in a medically induced coma and begin their program. You are intreavenously fed just enough calories to live. Trainers work your muscles as you sleep and tapes played in your private sleep pod help you to build better habits when you wake up. For an extra expense there are surgeries you can undergo, experimental techniques and more. Facial treatments, hair styling, skin peels, and more ensured that your body was at its best.

But the final result is what people cared about the most. With no effort, and no perceptible loss of time, people just woke up as their best self. They felt good. They looked good.

They looked better.

The extremely wealthy flocked to this solution in droves. People barely noticed when one of their crowd disappeared for two months, but they sure did notice the difference. Clients walked away looking twenty years younger, hundreds of pounds lighter, with radiant skin and perfect hair. And they knew how to eat better, how to maintain it.

And if they fell off the wagon, there was always a repeat visit.

If it hadn't been for the Vienna scandal, they would still be turning wealthy people into healthy people.

Three years after the founding of Coma Diet, facility in Vienna, the Viennese police discovered that they had been stealing sperm and eggs from clients. The news about the cloning experiments were the last straw. And that news spread all over the world, more quickly even than you'd think.

Suddenly the hyperwealthy started turning back to peloton and expensive gyms. And Coma Diet inc. had to pivot.

They needed to change their name.

And come up with a new business model.

The business model was easy to work out. Stunningly simple, really. All it required was one fully bought-and-paid-for appointee to the supreme court, a little R&D money, and, in the end, finally, one tiny genetics discovery that let them turn off developing consciousness in a clone.

That's the part they usually edit out.

66 - Retroactivity

In a way, this was paradise.

In a lot of ways, really. And it started with the people. No matter what the race, the species, the kind of person, they had learned to be kind to each other. This is no small undertaking. Many of the species that had come before had died out because they hadn't learned that.

And, yes, some had dealt with a meteor, but that was beside the point. It usually comes down to the people. They prioritized learning. They prioritized each other. They were kind.

So killing Waynescott was a big decision.

He was the first of his kind on earth in over two centuries. And he had gotten here through a time travel device that was certainly understandable in this time, but not really replicable. Which meant he came from the future, something he called an as of yet unrealized future - A future where giant bananas ruled the earth.

Marlo looked over to see if Marange was listening.

She looked up from her phone at him, "What?"

"I just said that he was from a future where giant bananas ruled the earth." Marlo was a bit annoyed.

Marange looked back down at her phone, "Well, that's stupid. Bananas are fruits. Or wait, they're berries, right?"

"Technically, a berry is a fruit, so it's right both ways." Marlo sighed.

"I'm guessing the banana thing was just to see if I was listening?"

"Well, you aren't. And i get it. I'm boring myself, too."

"It's not boring. It's just - everyone just assumes that the council will just let him go."

"Why do they think that? " Marlo asked.

Meringue set her phone down. "Come on, sweety. The council is not widely known for DOING anything."

"Well that's not true," Marlo swung his legs over the chair and tried to sit up straight now. He'd only been a part of the council for a few weeks, but he took that as a personal attack anyway.

"Sweetheart. You invent a device that can tell when disaster happens. It rings an alarm stating that it will happen in four days. Then, this time traveler shows up. One more hour to go. It's obvious it's him, just kill the guy."

Marlo sighed. This was all true. "Look, it's not that obvious to all of us."

"Why did you invent the Temparch if no one is going to listen to it?"

Marlo didn't absolutely disagree with her. He'd been working day and night to make it more precise. But he'd run out of time. Sadly, he pressed the red button on the chair. The ring around the televiewer went red.

Meringue looked up and kissed him on the forehead. "See? Was that so hard?" Marlo saw the cylinder containing the time traveler fill with mist. He searched the traveler's face. But the truth is, none of the people could really figure out what an expression on a human's face meant.

He took a breath as every ape across the world quietly disappeared.

67 - The Shadow Age

We name these different ages almost whimsically. Mostly it's the comic book authors who do it.

The 1940s were the golden age of superheroes. Brightly colored costumes and garish names like the Red Sentry, Helix, Rise, Glorious, The Grey Guardian, Godstar, Luminescent, Darklight, etc.

Many of them had no secret identities. Rise was just Jon. Later, he would become Omega and fight off the aliens, but back then, he was just Jon. Luminescent was a movie star. We were comfortable with our heroes.

And they smiled a lot.

The 1950s was the Silver Age. It was the rise of the Numina, ancient heroes. A little more secretive, but still our heroes.

The 1960s, 70s, and 80s saw the superteams gain prominence. The Echelon in New York arose, along with Union and Fourstar in Chicago. Ultra was the hero everyone loved. The Bronze age had begun.

The 2000s ushered in the Copper age. Nightwatch was everywhere. The Assembly became big, with Prototype, Machina, C-State, Purge.

Along the way, it seemed like the bad guys got harder and harder. Emil Zodiac and the Culling. Cavara, Ludeko, Allimirtis, the Front, horror stories, like the Arbettor Kon and more.

At the end of the day, though, it was just normal, non powered villains that were the most dangerous. Like Kuchin.

After a brutal recession, the nation of Laos had fallen into chaos. Commander Nai Kuchin had taken total control over the government and had himself installed as dictator for life. He acquired a nuclear weapon. And told the media that if he didn't receive eighty billion dollars within two days, he would destroy his own country and everyone in it. The explosions would reach Thailand and Vietnam and would kill over thirteen million people.

No leader had ever done this before. And it captured the attention of the entire planet as world leaders decided what to do. The superheroes all spoke out against him, too,

It didn't matter.

I remember it very well. Kuchin stood up on national television. The look in his eyes was psychotic. IIt gave you a chill to look at. He held the button in his hand. It looked like the nations of the world weren't giving in. They weren't going to give him the money.

He was going to do it on live television. He raised his hand.

And he just stopped.

In the coming weeks we learned more. Doctors said that his brain had just been shut off. It just powered down.

And, although no one took credit for it, according to experts, there are about fifty seven superheroes on earth who could do something like that. There are thirty two of them that could do it from anywhere - from any distance. And twenty seven of those were on the planet at that exact time. Twenty seven superhumans who could just turn off a brain from anywhere on earth.

So that is, people generally say, when it began.

That was the start of the shadow age of superheroes.

68 - Who is Jamie Carson-Roe?

"Mommy, who am I?" Jamie looked up at her mom with her lunchbox in one hand.

Her mother slid her phone into her jacket pocket.. "You're my little girl. You're Jamie Carson-Roe"

"Do you love me?"

Juliette kneeled down and framed her daughter's face in her hands. "You know I love you very much."

"Am I going to die?" She asked so matter-of-factly that it nearly broke Juliette's heart.

"No, sweetheart. You aren't. You are going to live for a very very very long time. So we should get ready for school so you don't spend that time as a dummy."

Jamie laughed. The darkness that had fallen over her face seemed to have disappeared entirely. She was just a little girl again.

A sullen red haired woman came from around the corner. "Oh. Ms. Carson-Roe."

"Principal Evans, how are you?"

The principal seemed to have no eyes for anyone but the little girl. She looked at her gravely., "Hi, Jamie, how are you?"

Jamie looked up at her mom, as though for permission to speak. Juliette held the principal in an icy glare, "Jamie is feeling very much better."
"We talked about this..." Ms. Evans began.

"And we agreed that this is the best option." Juliette was firm but kind.

"We can't do this every year."

Juliet pasted a fake smile on her face and shot back, "Ms. Evans, this year is the only one I'm currently worried about and I suggest you do the same."

"We have other children here..."

Jamie's ears perked up. "Oh, is Bobby Sunda here? I missed him."

The principal bent down and addressed Jamie, "No, sweetheart, Bobby isn't here this year. I'm sorry."

Juliette reassured her, "there are going to be so many kids here this year. You can play with someone new every day..."

"I would like that, mommy,"

Juliette kissed her, searching for some sign that she was growing up, anything that might suggest she was older now. Or that she remembered being sick, hurting. She saw nothing. She was just her little girl, the same as always.

"Please, Ms. Carson-Roe..." The principal trailed off, sith a plaintive look on her face that seemed tired, resigned. Juliette had always loved this school, but maybe it was time to find someplace more appropriate. Or maybe even more than one school. She realized that the world was open to her and her daughter and there was no need to play by parochial rules she didn't agree with.

She pushed past the principal and advanced with Jamie to the playground. It grew quiet, but the parents soon all looked away as their kids resumed their play.

It was just a few minutes of discomfort.

So, Juliet left her daughter in the playground of the kindergarten, just like she had every year for the past thirteen years, since the young girl had died in that exorcism and the priest had convinced the demon she really was the beautiful young girl everyone knew as Jamiie Carson-Roe

69 - The Wizard and the Change Engine

....

Tsanga was floating a few feet above the bed like she always did before bedtime. Geoff considered tying her down sometimes but then he figured, what would be the fun in that?

Some people born into chaos needed to swim in it.

"Will you tell me a bedtime story," She begged.

Geoff adored her and knew he'd never say no. "Why don't you float over here." They laughed while she drifted back to the bed and wrapped herself tightly in covers.

She started. It was the story she wanted to hear, "Once upon a time, when the world made sense..."

Geoff picked up, "There lived a young wizard. One day, he saw, in a portal, an image of the woman he was destined to love,. She had long dark hair and was so beautiful. He couldn't help but fall in love. "

Tsanga couldn't help but jump in, "But there was a catch..."

"Indeed, there was a catch. Because the portal had shown him the far far future. His heart's desire wouldn't be born for many thousands of years. So he waited."

"And he waited," Tsanga continued with mock seriousness"

"But he knew that in order to live long enough to meet her, he would need to stop aging."

"And that took power," the little girl intoned.

Geoff smiled, "That's right. Power. The wizard invented magic. Then he invented medicine. Then he invented the most powerful thing of all, the thing that generated real power. He invented Chaos"

"Chaos," whispered Tsanga, her soft blue skin radiant in the light of their two moons.

Geoff lowered his voice. "He created an order of chaoticians who generated so much power through the chaos they wrought that the Wizard could live on and on, for millennia. They placed portals all over the world, to inspire chaos. They grew people to great heights. They caused clowns to go mad all over the world. They changed everything"

Tsanga was so caught up. "changed"

"Finally, they created, with the wizard's magic, the Change Engine™. It changed reality daily, destroying the status quo, enclosing the world in chaos. This provided the wizard with all the power he needed."

"He would live forever, maybe." Tsanga chimed in.

"Maybe he would." Geoff winked.

"His chaoticians all died off or disappeared. But the Change Engine remained.

"And the powerful wizard, dreamed that night, but it was black. He looked into the time window but he saw nothing."

"Nothing at all," Tsanga interjected.

"That's right." Geoff continued. Because when the chaos came and everything changed, it caused the very rules of flight to change. And the things they knew as airplanes had come crashing to the ground."

"Crashing"

"Yep. Including the one that carried the girl with the dark hair. And the great wizard never saw her face again." Geoff finished up.

Tsanga whispered sleepily, "The end."

Geoff tucked her in tightly so she'd stay in place. His tentacles slipped soundlessly across the floor as we made his way to his room.

70 - At This Edge

....

"What do you think about babies?" Zack started while rubbing the small of Willow's back.

"I don't."

"You never think about having a babies - a baby?" Zack leaned back.

Willow rolled over, "You can't even pluralize it and you want me to carry it?"

Zack puffed up his chest to become mock imposing, "Look, womb, I got sperm I don't know what to do with."

Willow laughed and grabbed the pepsi from his hand, "There are socks for that, gummo."

Zack continued, "So you don't want a little me running around?"

"You ARE a little you running around, chicken legs."

"Oh my god, you are so black you call the police on yourself"

Willow shot back, "You are so white you're like a shrinky dink." Zack considered that. Shrinky Dinks were actually transparent. Not bad.

"You are so black, you're an antioxidant rich superfood."

"You're so white, Ritz and Saltines are fighting over you"

"You are so black your whole life is the rhythm method."

"That's not even an insult," Willow handed him back the drink and he took a swig.

"I know, I suck at this, I'm just looking at your ass. You're having a good ass day."

Willow leaned in, "Well. Looking ain't how you make babies, Matt Damon".

Zack paused for a minute, "I would like to have a little you running around one day."

Willow got quiet, "I can't imagine having the money for a baby."

"I can't believe I'm saying this, but we're rich in love."

"Oh, Skinny me Chalomet. Do not do that to me." Willow had been with Zack for over a year now and had not run out of ways to taunt him. "You're so beautiful I always forget we can't afford shit."

"Not even my good side."

"I'd love to have a baby one day with you, Justin Beiber looking motherfucker," Willow climbed onto Zack's lap and kissed him deeply.

Zack kissed her back. She felt almost weightless, but there was something about her, she felt more substantial today. Like something was more real. "One day, Tiny black girl. I'm going to find a place big enough to put a baby in your little body."

"aww. you never really took sex ed, did you?" Willow leaned in and rested her head in the crook of his neck.

Zack Whispered, "I did not."

They kissed. Not in passing like last time but the way you do when kissing is the purpose for the evening - it's what you want, the first and last thing on the menu for the rest of the night. Zack fell asleep breathing in the smell of her that he loved.

Willow got up and went to the bathroom. She pulled out the box and tried again, knowing it was just going to say what the last four did. She considered the seventy four dollars and change in their joint checking account alongside the two bright unmistakeable lines on the pregnancy test.

She let go and believed in love.

71 - The Woodshed of Second Chances

There are accidents in the universe that, almost magically, give you second chances. And if you are smart, you take them and you run, as fast as you can from your initial failure. You run and you make something better.

But that's not how all of us are made.

Donnie always wanted to be a superhero when he was small. And if he were one, his secret code name might have been "Second Chances."

Or that's what he thought, the 4th of July after his eighth birthday a firecracker had blown the tip of his finger off. He wrapped it tightly, more to hide it from his father than anything.

And by morning it had grown back.

Bruises, scars, it didn't matter. Donnie soon healed no matter what was done to him. It was as though the universe were giving him second chances, thirds. Even forths.

Maybe the universe felt sorry for him, Donnie thought.

Because try as he might to keep his father from finding out, Donald Sr. wasn't a man made to ignore opportunity. And after he brought Donnie out to the woodshed to punish him for ruining supper one night, it didn't take him kong to notice that the burn marks on his arms silently disappeared.

As though they were never there.

Donald Sr. was intrigued. The next time Donnie misbehaved, he dragged him to the woodshed and beat him. Only this time he took a kitchen knife and carved a circle in Donnie's back.

He wanted to see how this magic power worked.

And it did. Each attack on the boy was fully healed by morning. Even when Donald Sr. let his anger really out, as he did one day when he chopped the poor boys left hand off.

That took nearly three days to grow back.

The woodshed went from being a place of occasional punishment to an oasis for the angry, volatile Donald Sr. who beat and carved the boy up every time he had the chance. Until one day he bludgeoned him again and again with a baseball bat, his screams drowning out the woodlands sounds.

The boy laid there, unable to recover from brain damage.

Donald Sr. dragged the body, thinking without remorse how light it was. Donnie was ten years old when he had his brain damaged, the only organ on him that didn't regenerate.

How could he have known?

As he pulled the tiny corpse behind the woodshed to bury him, the sun dipped below the trees. Donald Sr. grunted with the realization he'd have to dig that hole in the dark. He lifted his phone and turned the flashlight on.

As his eyes adjusted, he saw the source of the noises in the woods.

He felt the weight of hundreds of desiccated, feral versions of Donnie reaching out, crawling all over him, pulling him down, each grown entirely from a piece of the boy he had left behind, bodies without brains, the only organ on Donnie that didn't regenerate.

72 - The Passion of the Xomla

....

"You seem sad."

"I'm just quiet. Tell me more about your world."

The Xomla reminded him that they didn't have much time. Kellen didn't care.

He wanted to dance.

He opened his eyes on the dancefloor and could feel his hands pressing into the small of the Xomla's back. This was better.

"You said it's cold, "Kellen dipped, remembering his youth spent on the dancefloor trying to impress various girls. The guys who were willing, at least, had a leg up.

"It's so cold, without someone to share it with. Being outside, being alone. It's cold."

"How do you feel here?"

 "You know how I feel. I feel complete. I feel warm. I feel loved. The question is how do you feel?"

Kellen spun the Xomla around the floor, "I feel like I want another hour, another day. I feel loved, too. I feel love. It's very strong."

"What's it like to be an astronaut? To be a traveler?"

"Is that what I do? I'm a traveler? So much of it feels wrong. To leave the cocoon of your own planet. To go somewhere you potentially aren't wanted. You have to get used to the idea that the place you are in right now was not made for you. It wasn't designed to keep you alive.

The environment doesn't love you?"

 "In a way. That's a good way to put it."

"We can't do that. We have to live somewhere that adores us." She stretched out the word "adore" until it seemed comical and silly.

Kellen laughed. "Are all Xomla like you?"

"In a way yes and in a way no. We're all really different personalities, ideas, philosophies. But we need the same things"

Kellen felt her energy throughout his body. This night felt special and he didn't know why.

The Xomla did.

"It's your choice day today. You get to choose. You have to, actually."

"Well, I choose you." Kellen felt so light on his feet. It's possible he was a better dancer than he even thought."

"I chose you already," The Xomla laughed.

"And I'm glad."

"You know you're going to die?"

"We're all going to die, Zee. But so few of us live"

"But very soon. You know that."

"It's worse than that. I'm going to die on Io. I'll be the human who died farthest from home of any man who ever lived."

"You really are a traveler."

"I guess I am. So how does this work, Zee?"

"You decide to keep me. My people are parasites, Kellen. We eat sentient beings from the inside out. We thrive on death."

"All species thrive on death."

"Your death. You will die"

"But you'll stay here, in my head?"

The Xomla smiled weakly, "Of course, Kel. I'll be here, dancing with you, we'll talk all night. Your body will disintegrate and you'll die"

"Now you sound sad."

"Maybe I am. Maybe I wish this part could go on."

Kellen smiled and dipped.

"Can we turn the music up?"

73 - Peace in the Purple Mist

It was not hard to generate enthusiasm among the Arbetter kon people for invading planet 624. The kon specifically made a point to name all neighboring planets with numbers so as to prevent their people from making an emotional investment. But the inhabitants of 624 were particularly loathsome.

Deep reddish pink and round, they looked more than anything like walking bags of organs soaking in reddish blood, packaged to carry home from the market in near translucent baggies. And when their ships first landed, they made short work of the meatbags.

The goal was to strip the planet of its resources and eventually destroy it, further enriching the Arbetter kon beyond all dreams. They were a fierce warrior race, powerful and quick to act. And they'd left a string of burned out planets in their wake.

And, as I said, planet 624 seemed like it would be no different.

At the beginning.

To understand what happened next, it may be important to visit the history of planet 624, an altogether unassuming planet that looked like many other M-type planets in star systems all over.

This planet had been around for over eight billion years before the introduction of the first fauna- the very first non-plant based life forms. If this seems longer than usual, it's because it is.

Most inhabited planets saw life evolve closer to the two or three billion year mark. The timing on this particular planet was a bit skewed, allowing the plant life to get comfortable with their surroundings, and to manage the peace of those surroundings well.

The sloppy rolling bags of meat and organs who lived there had never known war. They were easily punctured and killed and tended to defer to whatever challenge was in their way. They were a weak species, but one without much to fight about. Until now.

Realizing that their survival was on the line, the people of this planet began to fight back, to develop weapons and tools to send the Arbetter kon on their way. And it had caused them some annoyance, for sure.

But something else even bigger was happening.

As the Arbetter kon swung around the planet, they began to lose touch with their factions. More and more, communication between their leaders and generals fell to silence and their troops disappeared.

It seemed to those still in space, in orbit around 624 that both the kon forces and native inhabitants were disappearing. More and more they encountered entire swatches of countryside across the planet that were empty, seemingly devoid of people at all.

More forces came down from the ships, only to fall permanently out of communication as well. Time and time again.

And when the second and third waves of ships arrived, they found a completely empty planet, but one covered everywhere with that fine purple mist, a mist that became steadily more and more blue as the kon kept coming and the plants did what they needed to do to keep the peace.

74 - St Xavier's Bat

The motto, carved across the entryway to St Xavier's school for boys in Woolton was simply, "To make Jesus better known and loved," and it was well known all throughout Liverpool, England.

The school had been founded under the trusteeship of the Brothers of Christian Instruction by Jean Marie de la Mennais to educate and care for young boys. Many of the teachers were Brothers themselves.

Edward was not. Edward Linton was a legacy. He had gone here when he was younger and, as soon as he graduated and went on to college, he knew he wanted to return as a teacher one day - possibly even as a respected Dean.

Even when he was gone, it called him.

From hundreds of miles away, it snaked into his brain and opened his mind to possibilities.

And today, Edward made his way down the hallways of the prestigious school as though moved by powered wheels. He walked smoothly, briskly, without unnecessary movements, and he stood in front of the case holding the bat.

Visually, it was unassuming. It was a toy. A black plastic t-ball bat, paint wearing thin when it had been gripped so often near the slim end, filled with tiny dents and imperfections from use throughout the years.

But if you dug deeper, it was endless. It went on forever. He remembered the feel of the bat on his backside as he had bent over in front of the entire 10th grade class and taken ten blows from it. It hurt, but most of the pain was more than that.

In a school like St Xavier's weakness acted as a beacon, a clarion call to hurt and abuse you further. To be caught cheating or defacing property or lusting after another boy was to earn the wrath of the bat, delivered by the Dean of students, but the pain and humiliation didn't end there. It continued at the hands of the boys, struggling to discover for themselves what was right and wrong, they tortured each other daily for not complying with the ongoing shift of community mores and taboos.

Edward had felt the bat publicly more than most. And one year, as a second year, when he and a dark haired boy had been kissing near the back garden, he became an objective lesson for the bat. The dark haired boy sat right in front and laughed alongside the rest of his classmates. And after, Edward tried to forget the feeling of his lips on his as he joined in beating and kicking him.

And all of this pain the bat took in. it became larger than life. As Edward lifted it from the chase, he could feel its weight, increased beyond measure by the pain it had soaked up, the hurt and horror it had seen. It sunk into his hands and became a part of him while he turned and lifted it deftly over his shoulder.

And the bat drew him toward the boys down the hall.

75 - Dead Pixels

....

The police didn't care about the books or my notes. Which I can understand, I guess. The video of Jon killing himself seems pretty cut and dried.

It was conclusive they said.

But I guarantee you that I've watched the video ten times more than they have. And I know what to look for.

The whole thing is only two minutes and fifteen seconds long. But by the end of it, Jon is definitely dead.

No one seems to be interested in my notes, but here they are:

0:00 - 0:35
Jon talks about why he is making this video. He says he's scared but won't say about what. He says he has no one to talk to but that's not true. We talk every day. He's wearing a t-shirt with a stretched out v-neck, which is very unusual. Jon is always so well put together. Always.

0:36 - 0:49
Jon picks the rope from off the tabletop. It's already tied in a noose. There is junk scattered all over the table, which is, again, very unusual for Jon's place. He shows the camera in a way that seems overly performative to me in a way. For a second I can see his eyes darting to the left. I rewind it and I'm not sure. It could be my imagination but I think it isn't.

0:50 - 1:15

Jon steps up on the table and raises the noose over his head to hang it. For a second, his t-shirt lifts up and you can see burn marks- or maybe scars, on his stomach. I don't know what they are and the police say they didn't find anything. I asked them to look again but, again, they seem to want to just close this case. He hangs the noose and pulls on it authoritatively.

1:16 - 2:05

Jon wraps the noose around his neck and kicks the table away. This is where you can see it. To his left, on the table is a black area, hard to see because of the darkness of the room. But it looks like dead pixels. The table shifts and you can see the book he and I had been translating from Aramaic, open. Just for a frame or two, though, because the area over the book almost instantly becomes black. The pixels appear to die. Jon struggles and kicks some more. It is eerily quiet.

2:06 - 2:14

Jon stops struggling and dies.

2:15-

It's only a frame or two, but the camera seems to move. It's almost like someone bumps it. And you can see the book again, open, on the table, before the pixels die like the ones covering it before. It's only two frames, really, so that could be my imagination.

As I search the house for my copy of the book, I have two questions.

Why would the open book of the Mazzakin kill pixels on a video camera?

And what moved that camera?

76 - The Way of Penance

....

I write all of this now as a way of penance, a means of redeeming myself. It's set to post on Reddit when the time is appropriate.

When it won't matter to me anymore.

What's ironic is that her name was Penance, my little girl. Penny for short. Her mother died too young, but she had a gothic way about her. She loved the name.

I thought it was okay.

Penance.

It all started when she was six. I would come into her room and cuddle. I might take her clothes off and change her for bed. I might touch her a little, nothing dramatic. I never forced myself on her.

Until she was twelve. Then, I was in her room almost every night, wanting to "Dance with her".

I'm not proud of it. I'm a monster. I'm a terrible father and a terrible, weak, man. I abused her for nearly ten years. And then, almost ten years to the date from when I started, she climbed up to the attic and threw herself out of the attic window on the side of the house that opened to the cement driveway.

She cracked her neck and died instantly. The doctors told me they didn't believe she had suffered at all. She had been becoming more and more hysterical and the years went on, prodded, no doubt, by my incessant abuse.

And we all should have seen it coming. I should have seen it coming.

But I didn't.

Last year, as a form of penance, I began to read her diary. I would read a page or two a day, to keep the horrors of what I had done fresh. I did these things. But it was still hard to hear about them. She hated me. And she had every right. I'm a hateful, toxic man.

And I learned just how toxic from that little book.

I would hurt her, at night. But during the day, i would taunt her. I would say, "I'm looking forward to dancing with you tonight, little bug," In my best father's voice, knowing how her stomach would tighten and die a little.

I read about how I made her feel nightly. I read about how she tried, over and over again, to end it. And I read about how it was all my fault.

I finished it last week. This book that told my sin better than I ever could. It detailed how I had failed.

And that's why I'm here, on this boat. I'm afraid to fly, to drive, virtually anything. I know my time is short. And I don't know how it will happen. But I know you will get to read this when it does. How do I know? It's here. I finally got to the place where she died. But there is one more page. The ink is fresh and it's always dated yesterday, no matter when I look.

It just says, "I can't wait to dance with you again, Daddy."

77 - Deus Ex Machina

....

"All right everyone, Today, I have an unusual show. We are talking to C-State 17, one of the heroes of the Tech-Hero-Supergroup Assembly in Chicago. We're excited to have you."

"I am very happy to be here."

"So, let's start there. You're happy. You have emotions?"

"Yes, I do. That may sound strange to you because I'm essentially a machine. But emotions are very useful tools."

"Really? Because I just use mine to cry alone in my room on Saturday nights." Marc had a quick and easy rapport with the hero.

"I'm sure that isn't true. But it's funny.. And let me ask you a question. Your shirt. It's a very nice shirt, but surely you have other nice shirts. How did you decide which one of them to wear today?"

"Hm. I don't know that I did. I just grabbed one. No offense but I didn't think you'd notice."

"Exactly. Out of all the decisions you had to make today, that was probably one of the least consequential. So you used your gut."

"Yeah. This is also an audio podcast, so..."

"If you had to use your logic, your intellect, to make this decision, you would have wasted time. And forced yourself into expanding an inconsequential decision into something large and unwieldy. Emotions were key"

"Fair enough. So, emotionally how do you feel about Machina? She, uh, animated you. Is she a god to you? Is she God?"

"No. Erin is a kind and wonderful person who helped me be who I am. She is a hero. She isn't god."

"Erin, huh? So you do have some feelings?"

"Well... Invite me back one day, after I've figured it all out?"

"That sounds like I'm onto something. But, I have to ask. How did she do it? Do you mind talking about it?"

The supervillain team known as the Culling had created something known as the God Bomb. It was meant to incite a chain reaction in the atmosphere once it went off, destroying the planet. Erin... Machina, realized that the only way to stop it was to merge it with audio equipment, so it could be listened to and reasoned with, and an old stopwatch, so it understood the stakes."

"Wow. And then she convinced it - you - to not explode."

"It was not hard. She is very... Moving."

Marc's voice went up in excitement. "So, essentially you're half subway speaker system and half super villain bomb with a little stopwatch thrown in?"

C-State 17 laughed a little. It was a comforting laugh, one that made you realize he was a person like any other one. Marc realized that this was why he chose his show in the first place. The patina of self-deprecating humor let him be easy, relaxed.

"That is so true, Marc."

"Well, then," Marc Continued, "No need for 23 and me for this one."

At that moment, in the minds of the people at home listening, The God Bomb had finally been defused, once and for all.

78 - Night of the Subtractionists

....

Retconning is complex and not always intuitive. When a subtractionist removes some toxic element, person, or event from the timeline, it must be replaced by something.

It often feels to the casual viewer like water rushing in to fill the empty space left by a bubble beneath the ocean - once popped.

This particular bubble was an evil man. Insomuch as any man can be really evil. He was a failed businessman and reality tv star who was widely known for his scams, cons, and schemes, designed to move money from others pockets to his own. He was a man of short term interests until one night, he was made fun of at a press event by the president of the United States. It was on that night he decided to run.

And he did. He galvanized all of the worst fears and aspirations in the minds of his supporters. He made them feel impossibly strong in their hate. And through his constant bullying, he immunized them against cruelty, steeling them for the harsh realities of what would happen next.

The Temparch Matrix, the great computer composed of hundreds of real people, each with the gift of foresight, identified him as "The Mogul," a code name it would use for each incarnation of him in the timeline.

And each of these versions of him would cause irreparable damage if they succeeded at winning the presidency.

But as I said, removing his from the timeline wasn't as easy as you might think.

The risk of him being replaced, water in water, with something worse, was real. Also real was the risk of co-creation. The famous temporal scientist Dr. Augusta Tenille had written a book about it. When Subtractionists attempted to remove the mass murderer Nicholas Collandre from the timeline through repeated efforts it did nothing but make him stronger - virtually unkillable. Or the risk of affirmation, like the chase of the subtractionist caseworker attempting to steer James Blaser away from killing over one hundred people at a school dance, but instead, through her own death, had just inspired his curiosity for desolation.

There was a lot of risk here. And the Temparchs had a lot to fear about this.

Especially given that what they finally decided was so controversial and, honestly, kind of fucked up.

My part in this? I pulled the trigger. I was responsible for the removal. I was the ranking temparch and I take full responsibility for it.

When subtractionists confronted the Mogul at his estate in Florida, they went en mass. We sent over twenty men, to eliminate him completely from the timeline.

And we replaced him with a man just as evil. One capable of as much harm as he was, one who would inspire the same voters, the same fundamentalist nihilists. But this man, Vladek, had one key difference. In his head, nestled behind his frontal lobe, was a small tumor that was destined to kill him before he could do much harm.

So we hoped.

79 - The Lizard Queen

"Hi, Mommy, is that a gun?" Melissa stood at the bottom of the stairs staring at the dark-haired woman pointing the 44 caliber gun at her mother.

"A toy, sweetheart. We're practicing. Can you go upstairs and I'll be right up?" She smiled at her and flipped her blonde hair behind her ears.

The little girl nodded and raced up the stairs, her own long black hair trailing afterward.

"Unfuckingbelievable," the woman said, watching the little girl bounce upward.

"Please don't hurt her," her mother whispered.

"I'm not going to hurt her. Her name is Melissa?"

"Yes. She's good-"

"At math, yes, I know. I always was."

Melissa's mother stared at the face above the barrel of the gun. She looked so good it hurt. It all hurt. "What name did they give you?" she asked.

"My name is Sandra. Not Melissa. But she's my clone, isn't she?"

"It's all really kind of complicated," said the blonde woman.

"Well, uncomplicate it. Your name is Betina?" Sandra looked at her ID she had taken from her purse. She flipped it at her. "That name isn't familiar, but you are. Can you tell me why?"

"How long have you been following Melissa?" Betina stood up and moved into the kitchen. Sandra followed her, gun still aimed at her head.

"For about a month now. She looks exactly like me. She sounds like me. She's me."

"Not exactly. Do you want a drink?"

"More than anything in the world. But I want answers more."

Betina pulled the pitcher of iced tea from the refrigerator. She poured two glasses "You shouldn't be here. It's dangerous."

"As though in response, she saw the laser dot spring into focus square in the middle of Betina's forehead. She dove at her, "Get down."

Betina fell backward, pushed into the refrigerator. Her head snapped back as a bloody hole opened up in the center. Sandra scanned the ground for the gun she had dropped and half stared into the pretty blonde woman's empty face.

She found the gun where it had slid under the table. In all honesty, she had never shot it before. She reached out and grabbed it, her shoulder brushing against a small book taped under the table. Its cover was blank leather but, as she flipped it over, she could see a logo. It said LifeQuest. But at that moment, all she could think about was the clone upstairs, Melissa.

She heard footsteps coming in the back door. She somehow knew they would be in the mudroom by now. She made a break for the stairs and fell up them, staying as low as she could. She turned left into what she hoped was Melissa's room.

Sandra opened the closet door, her body covering Melissa from any possible random ricochet.

The little girl had been crying. She looked at her and said, "Mommy."

"She's not here right now, sweetheart."

Melissa took Sandra's face in her hands.

"I meant you, mommy. Is other mommy dead?"

80 - Hiro and Joro on the Porch

I"I know what you are, you know," Said Hiroshi between sips of lemonade, sunk into the overstuffed dark green pillow on the porch.

"I assumed you did." Joro slid the straps of her shirt down. On these lazy days when it was just her and Hiro and nothing else to do, she liked to look available, as though her clothes could just fall off at any moment.

"So why should I believe you?" Hiro looked at her from under heavy lids. It would be night soon and she might go. But as often as she did, just as often she stayed with him, here, on his porch, and it was wonderful.

Joro slid off her seat and crawled to him, smiling. She placed her head on his lap and spread the fabric of his robe to kiss him on the thigh. "You don't have to. We can stay on the porch forever." She kissed a little higher and arched her back. Hiro saw her silk skirt shift and gather at her waist, revealing the perfect globes of her ass, pointing into the air.

"My father told me about Jorogumo. That they can take the form of a beautiful woman, entice you, lull you in, and then kill you. But they are spider Yokai. They are deadly and mysterious."

"And my mother told me about men. They can be strong and kind and beautiful, making you fall in love with them. Their innate cruelty is drawn across their face, and they need that to survive business, the harsh world. But to a woman they think is beautiful, that dissolves like sand on the beach. And to see that is to fall in love."

"So you love me, little spider?" Hiro leaned back as Joro's tongue flit across his belly now, her hands on his backside, taking her time to reach her inevitable destination

Joro knew her ass was in full view and she spread her legs. She wanted Hiro to know that she denied him nothing. Her mouth came down on the core of him, taking him in.

She showed him what that love looked like. And then, when her mouth was free…

"You know I do."

Hiro felt it. He did. Over the past two years they had shared every kind of intimacy on this porch - this porch which shared the enchantment of his home, keeping him safe from monsters. But now as he laid his hand on her head while she eagerly pleasured him, it was hard for him to imagine her as a monster.

In his heart, maybe he did believe she loved him.

Once he was spent, Joro stayed where she was, her arms wrapped around his legs.

"Why do you give me everything? Is it to trick me off this porch?"

Joro was a Yokai and it was her curse to never be believed.

And Hiro was a man. It was his curse to have to know.

He held her hand and stepped off the porch.

81 - The Other Side of the Sun

Jaleel had been waiting almost thirty minutes to talk to the professor, but that was fine. He had some cleanup to do on the idea.

He anticipated some pushback. Denise walked away nodding quietly and he took a deep breath and put his paper in front of Dr. Jorgen.

"Nope," The professor pushed it away and started to pack his leather bag.

"Wait, wait, hear me out. This makes sense."

"No, it doesn't. It's a stupid trope and I specifically told you to steer clear of it."

"But I have an angle that I think you'll like."

"No, you don't. Because I don't like anything that has to do with the idea."

"C'mon, hear me out at least."

"Look, Jaleel, you're a good writer. Pick something else and do something great. Your parents are actually paying me for this advice. I mean, they pay the school, but they pay me."

"Ok, I have this really interesting way that they get there. To the Antichthon"

"Let me guess. They sit in orbit, wait for the earth to pass and stay in orbit around the sun for 182 days or so."

"How did you?"

"You drew a diagram on the back, genius"

"Fuck, ok, but that's cool, right?"

"Ok, one more time. Let's say there is another earth-like planet on the exact opposite side of the sun. And let's say that something has kept us from seeing gravitational perturbation. And let's say that no waves of any kind have reached us through the sun, which is just transparent gasses. And let's say the unprecedented fact that two objects sit in identical orbit happened.

And let's say your astronauts can sit in a tiny ship for 6 months there and six months back, with enough room for a year's worth of food and, worse, water."

"Yes. That does seem like a lot."

"Jaleel. Come on, buddy. You can literally write about anything. Why the Antichthon? Hasn't that been done over and over?"

'I've never seen it done like this. It's counter earth - yes, it's been done, but Ii can do it sort of post modern."

"So what are the people like on this other earth on the other side of the sun?"

"I think they're evil. What we think is good is bad to them."

"That's… Why aren't they just scared? Scared of how evil people are on THIS planet. They just want to live and be left alone, right?"

"They're more advanced than we are but only by a few years. So when we leave to go find them, they're here already. And they want to stop us from going there? How is that?"

The Professor shook his head, "No. I'm still not buying it. Why are they a few years ahead?

"Maybe they're six months ahead. Because the cycle had to start somewhere, right?"

The professor sighed and pulled the Teryon Generator from his bag, pointing it at Jaleel, whose body sucked itself inside out.

"Six months is kind of insulting."

82 - Vengeance

Mbala was considered the wisest and the bravest person in his entire town. He was well liked, for sure.

And when the rebels came to take all the children, he managed to trick them into leaving without a single one of these precious cargo.

Vikada, the rebel leader, admitted he had lost, fair and square. But that did not stop him from removing both of Mbala's arms out of spite with a machete before leaving with his troops.

The townspeople gathered and nursed him back to health. They were grateful for him, especially the parents. And despite his newfound restrictions, he still managed to be a lively and inspirational part of the town's day to day activity. He still managed to be happy.

People looked up to Mbala. His mother had grown up in that very town, but his father, an Egyptian, had disappeared not long after he was born, likely to fight and die in battle. Mbala could have looked at his life in despair. He could have been sullen and moody and angry.

But nothing could stop his powerful mind from moving forward, making a better future.

He considered the circumstances of his birth and knew what he needed to do.

So, he sacrificed and lit the candles needed to summon Sango, the god of vengeance for his people in the left part of his room.

On the right part, he sacrificed and performed the needed incantations to summon Petbe, the Egyptian god of vengeance. His mixed ancestry gave him permission, he believed, to consult with both.

As they appeared, he spoke to them with great deference.

"Great gods of revenge, I call on you both as is my right as a child of both nations. I am in need of vengeance, not just for me, but for my people. I wish to petition one of you to return my arms and empower me to seek my vengeance. But you are divine and I am only human. It's not my place to determine which of you is stronger. I am but an ant to you both."

His words in supplication pleased the gods. Some say they could see what he was up to, but it is widely known that the gods are not angered by the cleverness of their children.

Sango spoke first, "A test then, to see whose version of vengeance best meets your needs. I return to you your right arm, empowered to find and kill those who have wronged you. That is my gift."

Petbe rubbed his hands together. "And I return to you your Left arm, able now to heal and support your family and friends forever."

Mbala's arms grew back, both with power surging through them. He looked up at the gods floating in front of him.

"And, again, great gods, you demonstrate your wisdom in all things. For what is the power to destroy your enemies without the power to heal your friends, and vice versa."

And the gods were pleased, too.

83 - Kigali Night Lights

....

She was just a little girl back then, covered in dirt, hiding between houses and behind stores in the Kigali marketplace.

Ndongo moved with the sure footed speed of the merchants, darting in and out of the brightly colored wicker containers full of fruit and toys and lucky cardboard boxes filled with paper birds and rainbow colored note paper.

If you blurred your eyes it all ran together into a pretty wash of spectrum and movement, like a tapestry moving in a purposeful wind. She seemed a part of it all, just something that added to the authenticity of the moment, where the machinery of the Rwandan streets made it possible that there were wonders at every table, if you just looked.

She knew that her participation made the merchants' prices bloom so she didn't feel bad about taking the occasional apple, stowing it away in her bag for later, or gifting herself with a pretty piece of paper or two.

And sometimes, like today, there was the possibility of more. Ndongo found herself in an open cafe, her belly churning, remembering the meal she had eaten last night and how unsatisfying it was. On the chair, barely visible in front of her, she saw the small brown satchel, next to a pretty Igbo woman. She was dressed smartly as she looked around for something. Ndongo recognized that look, even at her age. It had always fascinated her.

She crossed over past the woman's table like velvet, and lifted the bag, sliding it under her shirt. She darted behind the cafe, hidden by the blue stripes of the canopy and felt her way through the contents of the bag, pocketing the money immediately.

The bag contained the woman's keys and credit cards, a small watch and a few pictures. Ndongo recognized that the former would be difficult to cancel and the latter would have sentimental value. She repacked them as they were once she found what she saw looking for: the plastic laminated ID.

She held up the ID and let the image fill her mind, creating a skein of webs connected to it from all over the marketplace. She had just discovered that she could do this and the lightshow filled her brain with blinking candle tips that looked, more than anything, like the holiday decorations she'd seen on the trees around the marketplace every year's end.

She followed the webs through the square and placed the purse at the end of it, on a chair in front of a young fruit seller in a deep blue shirt. He glanced down and looked through it, telling his coworker to wait for a moment as he rushed off to find the owner.

Ndongo could sense when they connected but wouldn't know what it was until she got much older, living nearly three countries away, helping people find what they were looking for from a storefront in a sleepy street, a matchmaker, a visionary, a lamplighter for the candle of love.

84 - The Job of the Shu Jing

....

Every tree in the Shu Jing has a story of its own and many span centuries or more. Each tree has history and a world inside it.

This one, cut down for lumber to finish his home, unknown to Quin Pac Lee, was once a man named Keiko, a man who had traveled far to solicit advice from the Shu Jing, and from the God Tree in the heart of the forest. He had sat to talk to the trees, giving in to their worldview, to their unique vision of the passage of time, and allowed his body to wind down, to root in one place, to join the slow spirits in their towering guardianship of the world.

And now it was Keiko's flesh and sinew that would build the floors of his home. It was his spirit that lay resident on the house, a red and white shuddered xie-shan on a hill amidst acres of beautiful Jiangsu clearing.

Kieko traveled to the site of the building in pieces, his body shaved into perfectly curved lumber with joints that fit together to a millimeter's precision, sanded and finished, ready to spread his spirit across this home and live again for centuries more as this dwelling, a shell that would house Quin Pac Lee's family for generations.

If you are not attuned to the spirits, this story will mean nothing to you. You will hear nonsense piled upon nonsense and care nothing about any of it. You will think it's absurd that we can talk about the trees as though they have a rich life, a soul that transcends their shape and follows them to the build of this home. You will think it's silly that we talk about the Jiangsu countryside and how there is blood mixed with the mud across this entire continent.

To talk about how a family native to this area was tortured by men crawling from Japanese ships, to convince their neighbors to give up their land, but also, as it is so often with human beings, to assuage their incessant boredom born from long eventless journeys across endless seas in tiny, featureless ships. And how this family's spirit resides here, on this plain, restless and hurt, blinded by their oppressors' brands, waiting to reach out and tell their stories to the people who would live here.

Or about the beautiful women murdered here by angry suitors whose patience had run short, monsters in the shape of people who murdered then buried their prey across these gardens.

Because that is the job of the Shu Jing. To be cut into strips of lumber, making up the floors of each of these residences, where they might employ their ineffable patience in the goal of listening. Where they could hear those spirits assembled across the entire country, so as to keep the peace beneath the homes of men.

To be the haunted so that the families of China would know silence at night amidst the whispering horrors below.

85 - Xenolith

···

It was a Thursday night when Joel came home from work to find himself sitting in his kitchen, eating a grilled cheese.

"What the fuck"

"Ah, Joel, you're home. I made one for you"

"Who the fuck are you? Joel had had a really shitty day already, which I probably should have mentioned in the first sentence.

"I'm Joel. You're Joel. Nice to meet you. Now, do you want a fucking Grilled Cheese?"

Joel had a hard time leaving work today. That was why the day was so bad. I'm sorry, I feel like I'm just making this harder. To make things easier, we'll call this Joel unemployed Joel.

Unemployed Joel went to the refrigerator, "yes, I do. It's my fucking cheese and my bread, man."

"Yes, but only because I didn't think to bring anything with me."

"What? Who are... What?" The other Joel thought for a minute that this inability to quickly process may be what lost unemployed Joel his job at the Fed Ex.

"Did you get fired today?"

"Not exactly," unemployed Joel flopped into a chair. He didn't want to talk about it. Not even with himself. "How did you know?"

"Huh. weird. Yeah, that happens." Joel handed him the grilled cheese, made with the crunchy parmesan layer like he liked it. But, of course it was like he liked it. This was weird.

"Are you from the future?"

"No. Or... No, I don't think so. I'm from a different alternate dimension. One where you dress better."

"Fuck you, dink."

"Ouch. Look, I have a proposition for you." Joel took a bite and stood up. "Hey, you want some hot sauce?"

"Yes, I want some of my hot sauce, motherfucker." He grabbed the bottle from his duplicate.

"Do you know what this is?" He tossed a small device on the table. It looked like a small keychain, attached to a rabbit's foot.

"It's a rabbit's foot. And yuck. Can you get that dead thing off my table."

"Not the rabbit's foot, stupid, the device attached to it."

Unemployed Joel looked more closely. "No idea"

"It's called a xenolith. It lets you travel between dimensions."

"Holy shit. Fuck."

"It's a game. I've been playing it for a while. You travel to different dimensions. The goal is to eliminate the Joel from that dimension. You take what they have. Or they take what you have when they kill you. Simple."

"Fuck you. Why would I do that?"

"Because it's fun, bitch. I have a million dollars sitting at home"

Unemployed Joel reached into the upper pantry and pulled out the gun. Pointing it at the other joel he pumped three bullets in quick succession into his brain. Once he got back from this other Joel's dimension with that million, he would have enough to to quit the game if he wanted. He pulled out his own Xenolith and pressed the button in the center.

Or maybe not, he thought.

He was starting to get good at this game.

86 - The Artiploid

Over three hundred men with guns were cheering the speaker standing on the makeshift stage in front of the Detroit LifeQuest offices. This one was round and red-faced and seemed deeply insulin deprived to Sandra.

She held the eight year old girl who looked, honestly exactly like her, on her lap and stared at Dr. Ryan over his massive desk.

"You won't believe this, but it's good to see you again, Rebecca."

The woman with the long dark hair looked into his face in disbelief. "So that's my name?"

She looked down at Melissa who had fallen asleep in her arms. "Is this just you being kind right before you hand me off to them?" she asked.

Dr Ryan came out from behind the desk. "Oh, those troglodytes? No. I'm not giving them anything. They can go fuck themselves."

"I'm out of bullets. I can't do anything to you. It's just me and her. No matter what you do to me, she's innocent."

"Rebecca, you may not believe this, but so are you." the Doctor pressed the intercom button. A man and a woman ushered in a disheveled looking man with a small black sack on his head. The two guards stepped out and Dr. Ryan pulled the hood from his head.

As his eyes got accustomed to the light, he looked at Sandra, who now realized she had to start thinking of herself as Rebecca. The man was balding and hunched over.

He stared at her face as though he was seeing a ghost.

"Oh, fuck me," the man said quietly as Dr Ryan put two bullets in his head. Rebecca covered Melissa, huddling over her.

"Shh shhh, it's ok. He's gone. The bad man is gone."

"What the fuck," Rebecca tried not to wake Melissa in her arms.

"That man's name is, well, was Curtis. He stole you from us, along with about eleven million dollars, I think. "

"So, I'm a clone."

No. and you aren't a blank. You are just a regular human being who also happens to be an Artiploid. Which is why those men want to kill you."

Rebecca realized she'd been holding her breath. She asked quietly," What is an artiploid?"

I suspect this is something you have figured out already. This girl is your daughter. She has no father. On this planet, there are about one hundred women who have developed the ability that we call parthenogenesis - they can give birth without sexual intercourse.

"Then why was I here?"

"You came to us and paid us to erase your memories. There is an audio tone that we use on blanks to erase experiences. But you didn't want to know who you were. You wanted to blend in. And escape them," He pointed out the window. 'And then this man stole your body and lost it before we could place you." He pointed to Curtis.

"They want to kill me because I can give birth without sex?"

"Yes. So let's talk about our counteroffer"

87 - The Filicide Judgement

....

"Detective, are you religious?"

"Counselor, how is that of any relevance?"

"I think you know." Reina realized she was leaning in over the table. She pulled her seat up and eased back in it.

The Detective was matter-of-fact about it all. "I'm not going to play these little games with you, Counselor,"

Reina looked at Judit, sitting next to her. She had been her neighbor since she had first moved in, over a decade ago. She was named after st. Jude, the patron saint of impossible tasks. Reina hoped that saint was paying attention now.

She put two photos on the table.

"What does that look like to you?"

"It looks like a child that was put in the oven. Is that what we're looking at, Ms. Romero?"

"No, talk to ME, tell me what you really see. You're a trained professional."

Detective Conroy took a breath. Sometimes you play their games to get what you need. "I see red and black skin, pulling away from the muscle, suggesting the child was subjected to a great heat."

Judit put her head in her hands. It was clear this was killing her.

The Detective continued. "Sometimes good people do terrible things. The baby won't stop crying, you don't get enough sleep. It happens."

"But that's not what happened here." Reina pointed at the second picture.

"What does this look like to you?"

"Why don't you tell me. It looks like bumps, areas on the child's head where he might have been abused in the past."

"But what do they LOOK LIKE"

The Detective lowered his voice, "They look like possible signs of previous abuse."

Reina pulled another picture out from the group brought by the detective. "And this, what does this look like."

"I've never seen anything like it. I'd say we should ask your client, Counselor"

"What could it be?"

"It looks like it might be a strip of skin cut from the child's back, still attached at the bottom." He drew that on the picture with his finger.

Reina was exasperated, "Conroy, come on."

"It's Detective Conroy.. Seriously, I'm not going to help make your demented case for you. This is ridiculous. Let me help your client here. The baby wouldn't stop crying, isn't that right, Judith? That's how it always starts."

"But not this time."

"What is your endgame here? Is this really going to be your line of defense?"

"This is the truth."

"Ok, I'll humor you. Let's say this is the truth. What happens if it gets out of this room?"

"I don't know, Conroy, I'm just trying to provide a zealous defense for my innocent client." She put her phone down now in front of him.

"What is this?"

"I'm her neighbor. I took this last week. Watch it. Or don't. "

Conroy picked up the phone, "What am I going to see?"

"I can't even..."

Conroy stepped out of the interview room and watched.

He hit pause as it rose up red from the crib.

88 - The Neighborhood Exchange

....

Stephen and Donna had heard about the local exchange from the neighborhood association, on a document they signed when moving in. They checked the box to participate.

They were good neighbors.

The new house was beautiful. They knew they would have to get rid of some stuff. The moving truck was practically the size of the house. But with the kids gone, it just made sense.

About a week after moving in, they had a basement full of stuff. So Donna suggested the exchange. It was simple. Whatever you didn't want, you placed it in a box on the front sidewalk. You texted the neighborhood association number and told them the value. You specified if you wanted something bigger or smaller.

And the rest sort of happened kinda automatically.

The next day, there would be a box right there, with something of equal value. Smaller or larger.

First up was the treadmill. Beautiful, expensive Pelotron. They placed it in a massive box that essentially blocked their walkway. And the next day, in its place, sat a tiny five inch square box. They opened it to find a lovely, expensive fitness watch. Donna placed it on Stephen's arm and he loved the weight of it.

After looking it up, sure enough, it was within a few dollars of the cost of the machine. And sort of in the same "theme," if you want to call it that.

It was about fitness.

They weren't sure how often they were allowed to participate in the exchange. Sometimes, when out walking, Donna would see a box or two on the front walkways of neighbors homes. But she never saw one being carted away or replaced.

One day when Jon and Sandy had put that breadmaker in a box and left it, Donna tried to stay up and watch. But she must have dozed off for a minute or two because it had been replaced when she looked again. And she never saw by whom.

But sure enough, the kitchen slicer left behind was within dollars of the cost. And the same theme, really.

Food preparation.

So Stephen pulled out the book. The book had followed them now from three homes. It was an early printing of the Bible. Worth a great deal, the internet told him, but most collectors had one. They had tried to sell it over and over again.

Stephen placed it in a box, along with a "steak of the month" club card, just to be kind. He fully expected no one would want the book, but, hey, everyone loves a good steak.

They both tried to watch that night. The fog had set low and Stephen had to walk out once or twice just to see if the box was there. In the morning, it had been replaced.

In a similar sized box was a book covered in ancient leather, written in some foreign language.

And what looked to be a living three month old baby.

It was not crying.

89 - The Never-Ending Wheel

"Here" the girl slid off the motorcycle. Amelie had been plastered to the back while they raced here. She looked down at the tiny drop of blood that had pooled on her arm, wiping it away.

Amelie looked up, "It doesn't look like much." She stepped into the warehouse door after the girl. Right inside the door was a cage on a table. In the cage, Amelie could see a small mink-like animal running, exhausted, around a wheel.

The wheel was rough on the inside like sandpaper. When the animal slowed, its feet were torn. Amelie reached out and opened the cage door. The cage had been electrified. Two minutes and a few shocks later, she had freed the tiny rodent and was holding it in her hands.

"What the fuck." Amelie slid the poor thing into her hoodie pocket, letting it peer out as it drifted to sleep.

The girl looked closely at Amelie. "That was the test. Nobody who had been through the procedure would have done that."

Amelie showed her her arm, first one, then the other. "You know I haven't."

"I knew. She didn't." The door opened and an older woman stepped through. "You passed. Hello, my name is Jex"

"Well, maybe you can look at my arms next time instead of torturing an animal."

"I'm sorry. We have to be careful. What we do is illegal?"

"What DO you do? And why is it illegal? I've never even heard of you people."

"Why don't you come in. And I'll answer all your questions. " They moved into the body of the building, filled with children playing together. Their families were there, too. And none of them had the 'x' like mark on their upper arm that showed they'd had the procedure.

"About one hundred years ago, an element was discovered in the human bloodstream. It was called Augerite. No one could figure out what it did. Until they tried removing it. Removing it made someone cold, compassionless, ruthless. Soon, all the wealthiest families had the procedure, removing their Augerite. Suddenly these children became powerful at business, ruthless negotiators, cold and calculating. They won, at any cost.

"That's what the procedure is?"

"Yes. and now, to even tell anyone is high treason."

"So, all these people here, they haven't had it done?"

"No, in this room are the last of the race of man who expressed compassion, who care."

"Fuck." Amelie looked back down at her arm and scratched.

"What's wrong?"

"I was at my ceremony. To have the procedure. They put a tracker in us now, just in case. There's a tracker in my arm."

Suddenly the entire room exploded into a paroxysm of activity. The families made their way to the exits as sirens roared in their ears.

"It's ok, it wasn't your fault."

"It was my fault. Please, run"

Jex turned and ran. Amelie slid to the floor, holding the tiny animal.

"Shhhh. It's going to be ok."

She rocked it back and forth.

90 - Intergalactic Affairs

....

Most people thought it was part of the entertainment when seventeen alien representatives teleported loudly in sparkly blue beams into Disneyland about twenty meters inside the front gates.

To their credit, none of the Disney management team seemed overly concerned about whether they had tickets or not, they just followed their instincts and fed them.

Three courses of funnel cakes, hot dogs, and tater tots later, the humans and aliens stood together in the atrium of the Avengers 5 attraction, the only building large enough to comfortably house the retinue outside the Fantasia castle, which was undergoing repairs.

"So, this tater is a tuber and it is cooked in such a way as to become a tot?"

"Exactly. But it's Po-tater." Liam had been trying to explain elements of earth culture to the diverse group of aliens all morning now. The chancellor, a large mucus-coated insectoid with a razor rimmed hole in the middle of his face, seemed as overly focused on food as his appearance would suggest.

"Po-tater. Well, they are delicious, and I am pleased they do not scream."

"Why would they... nevermind" Liam had abandoned most of his line of communication so far today. He was keenly aware that he could be eaten by any one of these aliens and it would not have been a visual surprise to anyone.

"This tour has been very enlightening," joined in the large red reptilian one covered in tiny roaming parasites. Liam was 100% sure he had drawn this guy one night as a supervillain on the floor of his two hundred and fifty square foot Florida mobile home as a kid.

"Disney has been everything to me, for the last twenty years. I honestly don't know where I would be."

"So, you believe that the Disney Administration fundamentally manifests good for its people?" The team archivist was named La-lo'edela" if Liam remembered correctly. She looked very much like tapioca starch. He tried to find her eyes to talk to her. His brain finally determined that she either had too many eyes or not enough and he picked a point over what seemed to be her shoulder to respond."

"I do." Liam was beginning to feel a little sick.

"Across the galaxy, it has become harder to find lawful regimes. We are glad that a viewing of the documentary film "She-Hulk" opened our eyes to your existence.

Liam wanted to address every wrong thing in that sentence but could not take his eyes off of the pink alien who looked like a pencil eraser with leprosy.

"Yay, She-hulk"

A blue skinned gel-like creature stretched to what seemed to be his full eight foot height and intoned with gravitas, "We invite the land of Disney to join us in the great pan-galactic court system," the rest let out a woop as his long purple tongue shot out and delivered a small boy to his mouth, stretched incomprehensibly wide. Seconds later, the child was devoured.

"And we will pay for that one"

91 - Saturday Night Ghost Story

....

"So you're telling us that you are the ghost?" Ahi asked, with the ghost stories book in his hands.

"Shhh. Let me finish." Kenjiro laughed and quieted the smaller boy.

Reiko jumped in, "I'm not buying it."

"I died on the way here, riding my bike. See?" Kenjiro lifted his shirt to show marks that looked like they were caused by the pavement, quickly dropping it again. Ahi considered that it all might be makeup. But he kept his mouth shut.

Reiko grabbed at Kenji's shirt, "Let me see that." The boys laughed a little and ran around the room until he gave up. "You're terrible at this. It's my turn now."

He grabbed the stick that meant that he was the ghost storyteller. He continued, more softly. "Kenji isn't the ghost. Because I also died on my way here."

"Stop it. That's not fair." For all the activity, Ahi was amused by the two older boys. They had gotten together every Saturday night to tell ghost stories. So far, this was the most animated one.

"My brother drove me here and was too cool to pay attention to the road. He hit something. And we died." Reiko looked up somberly, "I have no marks but my brain was damaged and the smallest amount of blood came from my left ear."

He pulled his long hair back and showed them his left temple where it looked like he had dribbled chocolate syrup in a small line running down his cheek, from his ear.

Ahi laughed now, "That's chocolate."

Reiko let his hair down again quickly. "No matter. The dead don't care what you think."

This last he said in his classic ghost story voice. A blue light was pumping from outside the window. Ahi looked into it. It was strange that he hadn't noticed it before.

"Ahi, are you paying attention?" Kenji called out to him. But the truth was that Ahi did feel a little confused. The air had a strange haunted feel tonight. He looked up.

"Huh?"

"I was saying that his brother's car hit me. That is why I'm here. It looks like we are both dead tonight. And you are telling stories with true ghosts." Kenji let his face fall into darkness in the room, illuminated only by the blue light outside.

"The Police are here," noted Rieko. They're here to alert your family to the senseless deaths.

Ahi's brain felt mushy. But even so, he knew that made no sense. Why would the police come here? If this were true, he would hear about it in school tomorrow, likely. Friends of the deceased don't warrant a police visit.

Did he remember when they arrived? He might have been downstairs, before the boys climbed into the window as they always did. But he had gotten this book before that.

This book from the top of the shelf.

Ahi remembered now, how he had climbed the bookcase and fallen, leaving his body behind.

That made more sense.

92 - The List

....

I think that making a list is the worst thing you can do to someone. It's like a cracked tooth, pulling at you, in the corner of your mind, every day. You see that person and you just think about it. In the cafeteria. In the rec room. It's hypnotic.

We've been gone for about three years now. But three years ago right before the ship left, a version of it from the future arrived. It was beaten up and contained the ancestors of the original crew. They told a complicated story that included the deaths of some of the original crew members.

After careful consideration, the United Earth Alliance decided to launch the ship anyway. We weren't told everything. But we knew enough to know that we wouldn't make it.

And I got the list of who would die.

I know that seems like a terrible idea, to release it to the population of the ship, so they didn't. But as the head of IT for the entire operation, it wasn't hard for me to access those records.

So many of us didn't make it. And the deaths were painful and haunted and, in some cases, extreme.

I was in the unenviable position of having a list, in my hands, of people that, as far as the universe was concerned, were already dead.

And so many of these deaths were inconsequential. The thing to remember about space is that it hates us. It wants to kill us and will take any opportunity presented.

Like the crack in Ramiro's viewport that sucked the air from his quarters until he found himself pulled, in tiny pieces, freezing and suffocating, out of a hole the size of a dime.

That would have happened in two hundred and forty days.

Or the engine room fire that Shohachi and Andrews accidentally started that literally cooked them from the inside with microwave radiation while the intense heat melted their living skin to the floor over the course of the twenty five minutes it took to shut down and extricate them. What kind of living hell would that have been.

in just sixty seven days.

Or the sheer brutality of how Irina Davies was meant to die, slipping and falling into the space beneath the hydraulic lifts that pump grain into the the silos, trapped for nearly a day while automated systems no one could stop slowly crushed her in tiny increments, snapping and grinding her bones down while her lungs filled with grain and each breath became a tortured wheeze.

Just twenty two days from now.

I hope that one day people will remember that I did everything I could do to alleviate suffering. When presented with an impossible situation, sometimes the only solutions are impossible.

I never would have thought I would become this, and killing my friends, even painlessly, has been the hardest thing I ever did. I hope for understanding and forgiveness at my own funeral.

In one hundred and seventeen days.

93 - Born from the Womb of War

Vikaro had been, years ago, a Jarl, and her blade served King Oggur, killing his enemies until finally, no one left to hurt him, he had drunk himself to death, peacefully, in bed, surrounded by his concubines and family. It was the death he had wanted.

Then, she was Jomsviking, committed to her brothers and sisters in battle through the félag that drew them together and forged their unique friendship. Her loyalty, now dispersed among her comrades, was no less strong, no less intense. She was six foot four inches of muscle and loyalty, built for nothing but supporting and defending those she cared for, no matter what.

Which was why today was so hard for her. Today she would fight for an idea against friends, companions she had known for longer than her previous self could have imagined. She was Kolubre now and it was her job to eliminate the unkillable ones who stood in their way. She stood there, in that red tent and watched one of them sleep.

Or not.

"You aren't sleeping."

"No, I'm not," responded the Wraith, his eyes still closed.

"You're waiting for me to tip my hand."

"I wanted to see if you were here to join me or stop me."

"There's nothing left to join. Unless you want to join us"

"So the Berserker is at the bottom of your ocean now?" He stood up and walked to the trunk, fishing out glasses.

"It's not my ocean, Jurmul"

"Call me Wraith. It's been my name for centuries now."

"And Silla. And Moran," Vikaro continued. "You are alone now."

"There are so few of us, Vikaro, And you've put so many now into the sea in your tiny metal boxes, to drown again and again until they're driven insane"

The boxes have air pumps to keep them alive for another hundred years. You know that." She took the drink he offered her. "We want sanity from our brothers, not the other thing"

"Why are you so attached to peace, Viking?" The Wraith took a drink and poured again from the bottle in his other hand. "We are Kolubre. We survived war again and again until death became sick of us, unwilling to take us. We transcended because of war. And now you and Yumma and the rest want to end war, as though that were something you could do."

"It is something we can do. In this century we're going to go public. We're going to tell our stories of war. We're going to change everything."

The Wraith suddenly threw his glass across the tent, shattering it on the floor. "You are going to change nothing. They won't listen. They won't care. They send their children to die - the things they claim are their most important gifts.They kill other children. For what, land? Flags?"

"I'm sorry that you won't join us. I truly am"

"The Wraith closed his eyes and took a breath. He knew he would come to miss the air.

94 - The Somber Ones

....

No one noticed her at work today

There were no donuts for her in the break room, not casual conversation for her around the water cooler. No one dropped off a stack of papers on her desk.

No one responded to her in the mirror in the bathroom as she put on her eyeshadow. Maybe tomorrow she wouldn't bother. Her email inbox was empty. No meeting requests. She opened her spam folder and noticed she had stopped receiving spam some time yesterday.

Mari confessed this was happening faster than she thought.

Oh, she had been prepared.

She had been mostly ignored for a good part of her life. Teachers graded her almost as an afterthought. She was never chosen in sports. Often she was just able to sit out the humiliating high school games, relaxing on the sidelines while other people took that dense red dodgeball in the face and fell crying to the floor.

The automatic doors at the supermarket seemed to wait, pensively, for her to approach a little closer than everyone else before grudgingly deciding to open.

This was how it was supposed to be.

You see, in various ghost stories, there is often a ghost, a character, who doesn't realize they are dead. They sometimes return home to their partner. Often their partner is reluctant to let them go, as well. Occasionally, the reunited couple lives together again.

In some ghost stories they have children - children who are technically half human and half ghost. These children are barely tolerated by the world. They are the somber ones. They never cry at birth. They never squirm when swaddled. They barely breath and only rarely speak up,

They grow up quiet, with few friends. They aren't special, have no great wisdom, and have no special abilities, except one, which manifests later. They work quiet jobs. They never know real love. They drift, they wander.

And then, one day, they just start to fade away.

Unless they do something about it.

And Mari had tried. She had sent letters to him, filled with flowery language. She had smiled at him in the elevator. She had referenced him in emails when she didn't need to.

But the letters sat unopened on the shelf in his cubicle. None of the smiles in that elevator were reciprocated. And each reference in every email was ignored with near religious commitment.

His name was Jerry and his hair was closely cropped over a firm, sharp face with piercing dark brown eyes. He wore bright shirts in purples and greens and powder blues. He laughed easily during meetings and made jokes that were actually funny, at no one's expense.

She stared at his cubicle from her desk.

After a slight pop, her hand slid effortlessly through the computer. It wouldn't be long now. She knew she would soon dissipate and leave this world. She closed her eyes and imagined, for a second, how it would have been different if Jerry had just loved her back.

95 - The God Bomb

···

"Oppie. Are you in?" Feynman snapped his fingers in front of the older man.

The four of them were tired and there was no down time scheduled in the immediate future.

Oppenheimer shook his head. "I'm just resting my eyes."

Fermi and Zodiac pushed the whiteboard back into the cluttered Los Alamos work room. In a previous life it had been a cafeteria and still housed a series of tables, folded up against the far wall.

Enrico Fermi had won the Nobel prize for Physics just a couple years earlier for his invention- Nuclear Fission. Today he was in a pair of shorts and a v-neck t-shirt in the New Mexico heat, moving furniture from room to room.

Emil Zodiac was one of the greatest minds of his time, as well. His research on nanotechnology was forty years ahead of anyone else. Today, he was tired. He was anxious to get back to the rubble of his life after the death of his wife. Everything he owned was in boxes and he felt adrift, empty.

These four men were entrusted with the hopes and aspirations of the entire allied forces. If they could perfect this atomic bomb, they could end the war, saving lives and preventing years of suffering.

Feynman turned to the two of them as Oppenheimer left to grab his notebook. Feynman said what they were all thinking. "He's a good man, but he's not us. He's not this..." He waved his hands at the whiteboard representing all their final work. It was a masterpiece.

Fermi spoke up. "Dick, what do you think? Will it stop? The reaction. Are we about to start a chain reaction that will set off every atom in the world?"

It was then that Zodiac saw it. He saw, on Feynman's face, uncertainty.

He didn't know. He scanned both their faces, these two men who were twice the scientist Oppenheimer was.

And they didn't know.

That was the day Emil Zodiac snapped a little. The day he recognized that the greatest minds on Earth, the smartest men and women this world had ever produced were just rutting animals infecting the face of the globe. He realized that he may as well have been a different species than they were. Which meant that as tortured and pain-filled as his life was, theirs was many times worse.

He saw that the only constant was pain. And that with even the most exultant minds a mediocre smokeshow, Humanity was mired in desperation

Zodiac turned to the whiteboard. With his immense intellect, it was clear that the reaction would slow and stop. He was unconcerned about igniting the atmosphere. He took in the contents of the board and closed his eyes, replacing each equation one at a time on the board within his head.

Until he saw it.

While it was clear that this bomb wouldn't destroy the world, he could see, in his head, the changes needed to make that happen.

He opened his eyes again.

96 - Where the Boys Go in Summer

....

Kokoru stepped onto the sand in her yellow bikini. Bending down near the water to grab her matching towel. She smiled at Chinatsu-San laying on her own blanket, in a black swimsuit. The two girls looked as though they might be related with their nearly transparent white skin and mops of black hair, moving in a sort of ballet atop their heads in the Summer breezes from the ocean.

As they sat now in the harsh sun, they kept quiet, their eyes fixed on each other, ignoring the throng of boys playing on the beach that day.

The boys, however, couldn't take their eyes off of them. Kokoru and Chinatsu-san were beautiful, for sure, and their bathing suits were thin and hugged their bodies tightly. Their lithe black and yellow shapes captured their imagination as the girls rolled off their towels and made their way, hand in hand, to the bay.

The bay was a private area of the beach, hidden behind towering plants and bushes, known widely for its seclusion, a place for lovers, maybe. The two girls swung their hands and smiled at each other as they disappeared past the thicket of brush and flowers.

They reached the foot of the pool of water collecting in the bay and stripped each other down. Aware they were being watched, they took time to play, to perform their striptease for the seven boys who had followed them.

The two girls turned now, nude, and asked the boys quietly to leave. They hadn't invited them to this spot and they wanted to be alone. The boys laughed confidently, much as a lion might when asked by a gazelle to avert his gaze.

They advanced as the two girls huddled closer. The boys looked wild now, inflamed as they were by the site of the two naked girls holding each other closely

Chinatsu-san's eyes turned black and her head lolled back.

The boys reached for them with passion, attempting to violently grab them. Each hand that seized one of the two women fell away, dissolving into the pool of water below. The boys began to panic and run toward them. But each footstep taken caused that leg to dissolve and fall into the water beneath them.

The boys cried out and cursed Kokoru and Chinatsu-san and each word was like gel, sealing their mouths until their faces were smooth and featureless. The seven boys flopped down into the pool of water collecting in the bay and began to shink, looking for all the world like tadpoles wiggling in the tide. Until they, one by one, swam off to the sea depths.

Chinatsu-san wrapped her arms around Kokoru and freed her, and she smiled slightly and dissipated into five small golden yellow birds, lifting off and taking to the sky. Her work here was done. Chinatsu-san closed her eyes to conjure up a new companion from other girls adrift in the sea of dead, silenced by these summer boys.

There were so many.

97 - The Way of the Bubble

....

We make choices every single day. Some of them are inconsequential It's rare that any of them come with a billion dollars.

"Excuse me." Rebecca thought she might have heard that wrong.

Dr. Ryan tried to repeat himself a little louder, but not loud enough to wake the young girl on her shoulder. "A one-time payment of a billion dollars."

"Holy... Why wouldn't you just kill me, right now. And take what you need?"

"Ms. Bridges. Have you ever heard of the story of Henrietta Lacks?" Rebecca had. But, in her mind all she could think was that this was the first time she had heard her last name. She was Rebecca Bridges. She should keep notes if she planned on having her memory erased regularly.

"I guess what I'm trying to say is that Karma is a bitch." Dr. Ryan opened the door to the lab and flicked on the lights. In the center of the room was the Bubble.

"So that's it?" Rebecca was expecting something more high-tech looking.

"It is indeed." He continued, "So, a one-time payment of one billion dollars, with a 'B', we protect you for the rest of your life, no matter where you live, and we wipe your memory again for you, if you like.

"If you wipe my memory, how will I know where the money comes from?"

"We draw up all the paperwork for you and put it all together today. Trust me, we're getting the better part of the deal. And one day we're going to have to prove we treated you well." He pointed to her daughter, "And your family."

"And then I can just forget all about any of this?"

"Well, you WOULD forget all about this. And the rest of your life would just be travel, opulence, and family."

"So how does this work?"

Dr. Ryan stood up a little straighter as he slipped into speech mode. "For the last decade, Lifequest has been leading the world in our use of genetic technology that helps people enjoy their lives. We learned to grow bodies, blanks, that let people live out their wildest fantasies. We've created genetic breakthroughs that extend people's sex lives indefinitely. Realskin covered sex robots, etc.

And now, this. The Bubble is a 3D genetics printer that can use cells - your cells - to create a pleasure body - a living partner with a viability span of a few days who will do whatever you like."

And my cells..."

"Your cells auto-replicate. That's why these mobs all over want you killed. You can auto reproduce" The doctor nodded to Melissa, asleep in her arms, identical to her

"I promise you. You, and she, will have a good life."

And Rebecca DID have a good life. She never remembered her deal with LifeQuest, even as the years passed and she grew older. But for the rest of her life she felt it, every once in a while, she never could figure out why.

She felt hands on her.

98 - The Death and Life of Angel Hansen

....

Sylvie was ten years old when Angel Hansen killed her for the first time.

The media had called him the Zed killer because of a letter he wrote to the Gazette saying that he would be killing twenty-six people.

And he would start with "A"

It was Sylvie's turn after Rainey Cutler had been found dead, stuffed in a box on the metro. Rainey was the eighteenth victim

Sylvie was abducted before the media even reported on finding Rainey's cut up body. She was number nineteen, petite and blonde and hopeful. Sylvie was a dancer and had a straight A average in school, even in math, which she just knew she had to work harder at.

By this time, the police knew his name.

And Angel Gerrold Hansen had disappeared. Impossibly, no one in the Midwest had seen him now for years, despite the fact that he kept on killing.

The first time he carved Sylvie up, he explained how he would torture her. He pulled, from his pocket, a tiny metal cylinder. It had strange engravings all around it. Angel Hansen called it "The Gish" and claimed he had won it in prison in a card game.

He discovered that the device had unusual properties. When placed upright in a room, no one in that room could die. Oh, they could be hurt. But any wound would heal. And even if it were catastrophic, it would soon be undone.

Angel Hansen placed the Gish on a table right outside the cell.

And then he tore Sylvie's head off.

She felt him twisting her head, as though it were the top to a mason jar. Until her bones snapped and the skin stretched and tore. She remembered, for a split second, looking out her own eyes and watching her decapitated body drop to the floor.

The next day, she woke nearly stuck to the floor in her own clotted blood.

From that moment on, every day, Angel Hansen visited her to kill her over and over again. He called her his favorite. And every time she died, she felt a little more inured to the pain. Oh, it still hurt, but every day she realized a little more than pain itself went away. The horror of it all no longer consumed her. And her only thought was to escape.

The day came that Angel had promised. The day he would take a mallet and crush her dancer leg bones to powder. He was so excited to take her legs away. He lifted the mallet and brought it down again and again until the thin skein of her skin was the only thing holding her legs together. And then he turned his back. And she leapt up and strangled him to death with her rubber-band-like legs.

So when, out of the blue, Angel Hansen returned almost thirty years later, kidnapping poor Alicia Hamwell. Sylvie's heart started pounding.

How could Angel Hansen be back?

When she had the Gish in her pocket.

99 - 'Yar Kwamfuta

....

Dr. Nibari transported onto the darkened bridge of the ship, arms filled with metallic cases. A vision of the serenity of spacedock seventeen could be seen out the port viewer, with so little activity that it may as well have been a still image.

The doctor felt that calm come over her that she had always identified with being on this ship. It was her final placement as Ship's doctor and the place she had learned patience.

She had taken this assignment after the accident that had separated her and her sister. While serving on the Unification, Abira broke into the engine deck and managed to shut down the runaway nuclear reaction before it destroyed everyone. The Dr. was unable to save her life. And she died a hero, having literally pulled thousands of people from death's door.

The doctor applied every bit of insight she had, both in biology and in neurologic systems and transferred her sister's consciousness to a computer.

That computer eventually became the onboard logistics computer for the Wilmont, the ship beneath her feet right now.

As she opened the cases and began the assembly she thought about all the time she had spent reconnecting with that computer voice, cautiously, carefully prodding it to remember. She searched the voice's tone for signs of trauma and then continued, every day, rebuilding the trust and restoring their relationship.

The pieces snapped together easily as she had designed them

to. It was surprisingly light, but sturdy. The Doctor's fingers
felt for the joints and enclosures that only she knew were the
re

Doctor Nibari then added the final touch. She pulled the locket from
around her own neck and slid it over the head of the robotic body in front
of her, The picture of her sister stared back at her.

She stepped back to appreciate the beauty of it. It was blue-black and
chrome with a deeply expressive face. The eyes were a dark brown, as
they had always been when she was alive.

She called out in the silence of the ship, "'Yar Kwamfuta"

Suddenly the bridge was alive with tiny lights and a warm hum. The
computer responded.

"Sister. I'm so happy you're here. Computer Girl, reporting for duty," She
laughed. Long before she had died in that accident saving her ship, Abiri,
young and bright and always with some technology in her hands, was "'Yar
Kwamfuta" - Computer Girl.

Now, that computer voice was giddy with excitement. She knew what
today was.

As the familiar voice washed over Dr. Nibari like waves of joy, she
explained the procedure. But they had talked about it thousands of times
when she served on board the ship.

It was an excuse to talk.

She smiled at the body she had brought, one that would house her
beautiful sister and take her everywhere she wanted to go, so similar to
the one the doctor herself now wore, hundreds of years after they had
last hugged.

And she flipped the switch

100 - Outside the Backstage Door

....

Willow waited for a good ten minutes outside the theater, which was ten minutes longer than she had ever waited for anything. The door finally opened.

"Hi. You were so good. I've seen the show like 4 times already."

Zack almost tripped over her feet, "Wow. really? That means... Wow." He took the picture she held out.

"it's dumb, but I drew this of you."

"Oh my god. This is... you drew this?"

Will stood up a little taller, "Yes, it's black marker pen. Acrylic"

Zack looked back and forth from the beautiful single line drawn image in his hand to the stunning onyx face of the girl in front of him.

His smile felt so much dimmer to him now that he'd seen hers. "I love it.

Willow stared at him over the picture, "You are a really great actor - and musician."

Zack was taken aback a bit by all this. It hadn't been a very good night until now. "Well, thank you for thinking that. Is that lame? I appreciate this so much. You are a really great artist."

"You think so? You like it?"

"Amazing. I mean, you're a really great artist, I'm a pretty good actor, we could be, like, brutally poor together. "

Willow responded in a false matter of fact tone, "We'd have to be."

"True true. Hey, you want to go get a small and cheap cup of coffee?"

"Will it be bad, too?"

Zack had thought he should add that to the qualifiers. "Almost definitely, but you can put stuff in it."

"Like sugar and cream and meth?" Zack had tried to put the picture in his coat. Willow jumped in, "Oh, just fold it, sad Drake."

"Hm," Zack tried to remember how much he had in the bad coffee fund in his Capital One account.

"I warn you, I throw up easily."

"Nice. Now this night is picking up."

Willow chucked him in the arm, Oh, shut up, Twinkie Macbeth"

Zack smiled at her, "Should we order a bucket, too?"

"We should get two."

"Whoa," Zack countered. "I don't throw up."

Willow grabbed his arm and stepped over the pothole in the alleyway, "They're both for me. What if i need to pee, too?"

"So, just like, pouring out of both sides?"

"That's how I do."

"Thanks for the heads up." Willow's hand was smooth and warm on the back of his arm and she was close enough now that he could smell her. She smelled like what Zack imagined would be an expensive desert cart tray.

He laughed, "This is the most romantic date ever."

"Virgin," Willow shot back.

"For sure. I'm probably a priest."

"Maybe I should be a little boy."

Zack looked over and laughed, "Not with that rack, SZA"

"So we all look alike to you?"

"By alike, do you mean fine?"

And in the dark of the alleyway, as they made their way to the coffeeshop, it became harder and harder to tell whose laugh was whose.

THE END